Kissed by Eternity

The Sunwalker Saga, Book Six

Shéa MacLeod

DEDICATION

This final installment of the Sunwalker Saga is dedicated to you, my readers. Thanks for joining me (and Morgan!) on this amazing journey over the last three years. Part of me is sad to see this chapter of the Saga end, but part of me is crazy excited about what comes next! Because the world of the Sunwalkers doesn't end here...

Shéa MacLeod

Chapter 1

A bomb exploded to my left. Dirt and debris shot into the air before peppering the ground. A clod of dirt smacked the top of my head. Damn, that stung. But I didn't stop to check for damage.

I ducked and dodged to the right as another explosion rocked the high desert. One of the Sidhe Queen's men appeared in my line of sight, his armor glinting in the late afternoon sun. I felt the Darkness stretch my lips into a feral grin as I raised my hand, palm outward. He'd never know what hit him.

Something slammed into my side, and I crashed into the hard earth with enough force to rattle my teeth. I let out an animal scream and reached inside me for the Fire, prepared to unleash its fury on my attacker.

"Oh, no you don't, Morgan Bailey." Kabita Jones, my best friend and boss, grabbed my hand. "I like my skin the way it is, thank you."

"Kabita. What the heck?" I hauled myself slowly to my feet. "I was just about..."

"Yeah. I know. You were just about to send an icicle through that Sidhe's heart. Then where would we be?" She gave me a stern look, reminiscent of my mother. Her long, black hair was bound in a tight braid, and she was wearing her usual demon-hunting outfit of black jeans, black shirt, and black leather jacket and boots. Her brown eyes snapped angrily.

I stared at her, baffled. What was her freaking problem? I opened my mouth, but she interrupted before I could speak.

"Do you know what would happen if you got involved in this war?" She ducked as a djinn-thrown fire spear sailed overhead, burying itself in the ground inches from a Sidhe warrior. The Sidhe yanked the spear out of the ground and lobbed it back. "You take sides, and all bloody hell really will

5

break loose. Whichever side you pick, the other side is going to rain hellfire down on humans. We'd never stand a chance. Do you want that?"

"No," I shouted back over the whistle of incoming crossbow bolts. "But I can't let this stand. The queen can't attack the djinn and get away with it."

"Then you better figure out another way."

I opened my mouth to tell her I couldn't, then stopped. Maybe there was a way. "Um..."

"What?" She lifted a brow.

I'd never told Kabita about my trip into the Otherworld — aka fairy land— with Jack a few weeks back. Jack, Sunwalker extraordinaire and pain in my backside, and I had been tracking a prison escapee when we'd ended up in the queen's court. I'd never mentioned how I happened to discover I could use my Earth power to control the denizens of the Otherworld. It wasn't something you spread around unless you wanted to end up extremely dead. Besides, I'd never tried it on this side of the portal. It might not even work.

"I might be able to control some of the Sidhe."

"What?" Kabita shrieked. "Since when? Why didn't you tell me this before?" She looked like she wanted to strangle me.

"It doesn't matter. I don't know how much I can do. I mean, I've controlled a small fey creature before, and from the reaction I got, it seemed to be a sign I could do more." That was the understatement of the century.

"Then do it!" she howled. "Make those damn fairies stop this shit."

"I can't control the queen. Maybe her soldiers," I admitted. "But then what? The minute I stop the fighting, the djinn will slaughter them. How is that any better than me outright fighting?"

"Shit." Kabita rarely swore, which meant we were in deep

doody. She rubbed her forehead. "It's not."

"Exactly."

"Wait." She yanked me to the left as another volley of bolts streaked by. There was a howl as at least one of them hit their mark. "What if you marched them off djinn lands?"

"The djinn may be tied to this land, but the Marid is the only one who can't leave. The rest of them can just keep on fighting."

"Damn."

"Exactly. Any other brilliant ideas?"

She scowled at me. We both ducked as another explosion shattered a nearby juniper tree. Splinters shot everywhere. "What if you forced them back into the Otherworld?"

"I'd need a portal, and only the queen can open one. I'm pretty sure she's not going to do that because I ask nicely. Besides, have you forgotten? I may be able to control the Sidhe, but the Marid can control me." Or rather, my Air powers. He'd done it before when they'd gone out of control. It had been for our mutual benefit that time, but who was to say he couldn't use it for his own purposes? The last thing we needed was the Marid using me to fight the Sidhe.

"Dammit," she snarled, chewing on a fingernail. "There has got to be a way."

"There is always a way," said a calm voice.

We turned to face the newcomer. Tommy Wahenaka. He'd been my father's friend and was now my training guru. I sure hoped he was right.

"Tell me," I said. "We need to end this before anyone else dies."

"Why do you care if the Sidhe die? Or the djinn?"

"Excuse me?" I snapped.

Tommy stared at me serenely. The wind teased strands of long white hair that had escaped from his double braid. He leaned on a walking stick of twisted wood worn smooth by time and handling. "Why do you care? This is not your fight, Morgan Bailey." He eyed me intently, awaiting my reaction.

"How can you even say that?" I gaped at him. "This is my fight. Morgana made it my fight when she used me to start this war. Why should their people die because Morgana and the Marid are having a tiff? And now it's not just about djinn and Sidhe. Humans are at risk, too."

"Morgana used you, yes," Tommy agreed. "But the Marid allowed his pride to control his actions. And Morgana would have used another excuse to attack the djinn. This has been generations in the making. All you can do is protect your people. Our people."

"But I don't know how. Other than stopping this war." And I didn't. My brother, Trevor, already had his agents from the SRA —the Supernatural Regulatory Agency— surrounding djinn lands with guns. Not that conventional weapons would work on the Sidhe anyway. Probably wouldn't harm the djinn much, either. They were there because they had to be. It was all we could do. I had nothing. I was a Hunter. I killed vampires for a living. This was way beyond my pay grade.

"Very well," Tommy said. "You've been given your gifts for a reason, Morgan. Reach inside. You'll know the answer. What power can you use that neither djinn nor fae can breach?"

I winced as another explosion rocked the ground. More dirt and debris shot in the air, raining down on us. It peppered Tommy's long hair. He plucked out a sage branch, completely unruffled, and dropped it on the ground.

"Darkness," I said. It was the only thing that neither djinn nor fae could connect to, nor did they have particular defenses against it. Not like Fire. Or Water. Although those might come in handy, too.

"Use it. Bind it to your other powers and use it to contain

what's inside."

"I don't think I can do that all on my own."

"You don't have to," Kabita said grimly. "I can set wards, and you can attach your power to each one, magnify it. I'll erect a circle, creating a barrier to contain the battle. You use the wards to channel the Darkness into the circle. They won't be able to breech it." Kabita was Witch Blood, a natural born witch, in addition to being a demon Hunter. Setting wards would be a piece of cake for her.

It made sense mixing witch magic with my own powers. Tommy was right. There was another way. I could only hope it worked. "Let's do it."

We started where we stood. Kabita knelt on the hard ground to place the first ward. She traced a pattern in the dust and whispered a few words over it. I could almost feel the energy she was pouring into it, static electricity raising the hair on my arms. As she spoke the last word, the design sank into the earth, leaving no trace. All I could see was a faint glow of energy where it had been. Kabita stood and gave me a nod.

With the ward ready to go, I placed my hand on the faintly glowing ground. I felt the zingy energy that was one of Kabita's spells. I tapped into it, letting it flow into me as I sent the Darkness curling down from the center of my being into the energy of the ward. Once it was done I straightened.

"Now where?"

"This is going to be a huge circle. We'll take my motorcycle. It can handle the terrain. We'll place a ward every couple hundred feet or so."

Tommy watched as we climbed aboard the sleek, black Harley. Neither of us bothered with a helmet. The magic would kill us long before falling off a bike would. With a wave to Tommy, Kabita revved the bike and took off through the high desert. The rough terrain jostled us, each bump and pothole jarring my spine and rattling my teeth. I made a mental note to never allow Kabita to drive me through the desert on the damn thing again.

She pulled to a stop and kicked down the stand. Once the second ward was set and I'd channeled the Darkness into it, we took off again. Rinse and repeat. We placed wards until the entire battleground was enclosed. Meanwhile the SRA agents held the line, albeit with some difficulty. I was fairly certain Tommy was helping. In his way.

Back at the first ward, Kabita began the ritual that would link the wards together, creating a circle of power the violence could not cross. The Sidhe would be able to leave, but once they exited the circle, they couldn't return or bring enforcements, and the djinn would be stuck behind the barrier unable to leave at all. This was their land, after all.

As Kabita continued with the ritual, I continued pouring my Darkness into the ward. Then with a final command, the circle snapped shut. My Darkness raced through the wards one at a time until each was linked. While my physical eyes saw no change, my sixth sense, my third eye, could see the dark dome of power encompassing the battle. A pair of warriors, locked in combat, crashed into the side of the dome. Electric sparks shot up across the invisible barrier, but it held. The two crumpled to the ground as if they'd hit a brick wall. Shaking their heads slightly, they staggered to their feet and went at it again.

I breathed a sigh of relief. "It worked."

"Of course it did." Kabita seemed offended I'd doubted her.

"I was thinking of my part in it," I said apologetically. "You know me and my freaky powers."

I watched the battle inside the dome. It raged on, but the sound was muted as if watching on a TV with the volume on low. Blasts of power flew left and right but hit the walls and dissipated. As long as the wards held, humanity would be safe.

For now.

Kabita's phone chirped. She glanced at the screen. "I've got to get back to Portland."

"You can't go," I insisted. "I need you to make sure the wards hold."

"They'll hold. At least for a while."

I shook my head. "This is Sidhe and djinn power." The dome shuddered as if in response to my doubt. "You have no idea how it'll react."

"I've held more demons inside one of these than you can shake a stick at."

"But adding the Darkness..."

"There's a demon infestation in a church of all things. Do you want them eating the Sunday school kids for breakfast? I have to go."

Tommy grabbed my arm. "Go," he told Kabita. "We can hold it."

She nodded, and without another word hopped on her bike and took off. I whirled to Tommy. "I hope you're right because I'm not convinced." The dome shuddered again as another ball of Sidhe energy slammed into it. The SRA agents fell back, watching the battle. I'd bet anything they were confused as hell right now.

"We must," Tommy said. "She cannot allow more death simply because of what might happen here."

He was right. "Does shaman magic even work on a witch ward?" I asked.

He smiled grimly. "I guess we'll find out."

Chapter 2

I saw the minute the ward began to flicker. "Shit, I think it's dying," I shouted to Tommy. He was several feet away at the next ward. He jogged back, his spry movements belying his age. He knelt down, hands extended, searching for the power in the ward.

"Kabita's magic is collapsing. There is too much strain on the barrier."

No shit. Somebody crashed into the invisible wall, causing it to shudder and spark. The djinn staggered to his feet, shook his head, and dove back into the fray. Nobody on the battlefield seemed concerned there was an invisible wall keeping them inside.

"What do we do?" I was trying really hard not to think about what might happen if the wards failed.

Another body hit the wall. This time an entire section went down, spilling the fighters out onto the ground. Fortunately, the rest of the barrier was still intact for now.

"We need to close the gap before more escape, that's what we need to do," Tommy said grimly.

"But how? My power isn't helping anything." The Darkness could keep the beasties at bay, but it couldn't charge the wards. And Tommy was doing his best, but apparently shamanic power worked differently than witch power.

He placed his hand on the ward and concentrated. I could almost feel the energy pulsing from him, charging the air. The ward throbbed faintly, and the wall shimmered, restored. I knew it wouldn't hold for long, though.

Tommy glanced at me. "Look out!"

Somebody grabbed my hair, yanking me backward. My first instinct was to fight, but instead I let myself go limp, falling back so my hair slipped out of my captor's grip. Tears stung my eyes at the pain on my scalp. I hit the ground and rolled toward my would-be captor, sweeping my right leg around until it slammed into his legs. He hit the ground beside me hard enough to knock the wind from his lungs. The sun glinted off golden armor: Sidhe.

I slid my blade from my boot and lifted it, prepared to make the death strike. It was the blade I'd liberated from the Otherworld. It would slice through Sidhe armor like butter.

"Morgan! No!"

I glanced up to see Jack running toward me across the uneven ground. A djinn rushed him only to receive the hilt of Jack's sword in his temple for his trouble.

Instead of making the blow, I pressed the blade against the Sidhe warrior's throat. He immediately stopped struggling. "Jack? What the hell are you doing here?" I hadn't heard from the bastard in days. Not since Paris. He hadn't returned my texts, calls, or emails. When I'd needed him most, he'd disappeared off the face of the earth. Worst guardian ever.

"Don't kill him," Jack ordered. "It's what the Queen wants."

I stared down at the warrior, who was staring up at me. The swirling permutations of his features made me a little dizzy. "I know that, Jack. I'm not an idiot."

He raised an eyebrow, which irritated me. I did know that, but in the heat of the moment, I'd forgotten. Or rather, I hadn't cared.

"What do you propose we do with him?" I glanced over at a djinn who was lying prone just outside the barrier. "And that one. We can't let them run amok."

"Trevor just brought in a cage. We can throw them in there."

"Both of them?" Tommy and I said at once.

"Don't be an idiot," I said. "They'll kill each other."

"Djinn can't die, Morgan. Neither can Sidhe."

"Djinn and Sidhe can't die at the hands of humans, but they

can sure as hell kill each other."

"Shit."

"Exactly."

"Why don't we put one of them in the cage," Tommy suggested, "and tie the other up. Iron cuffs will hold the Sidhe. Especially if they've been charged with power. The djinn will be trickier."

We were halfway to the cage when the barrier went down again. I could tell by the fizzle and the black smoke it was done. There was no bringing it back. The wards would have to be completely reset.

Warriors poured through the gap, carrying the battle outside the dome. The djinn lunged out of Jack's grasp, snapping backward with his elbow and catching Jack in the nose. Blood spurted everywhere as Jack staggered to the side. Tommy wacked the djinn in the head with his staff, driving the larger man to the ground. The Sidhe I was holding took that moment to decide running was a good idea. He twisted wildly to the left, breaking my hold, then took off toward his brethren and the battle. I snatched up a fist-sized rock, and channeling a bit of the Darkness, lobbed it after him. It hit the back of his skull, and the Sidhe went down like a ton of bricks. He didn't get back up.

"Now what?" I shouted at Tommy and Jack who were trying to restrain the djinn. It looked like a losing battle. The thing was massive, and he was tossing them about like they were children. "There are too many of them."

Warrior after warrior poured out of the dome. Blood splattered what was left of the invisible barrier, hanging in midair like a gravity-defying painting of the macabre. Another ward sizzled and failed, giving the fighters even more room to spill out. Soon they'd cross djinn territory onto human lands. Then we'd have a serious problem.

"Use your powers," Tommy shouted, giving their captive

another whack with his staff. The djinn fell to his knees, dazed.

I scrambled for an idea. If I used Air, the Marid could control me. If I used Earth, the Sidhe would be unaffected. Water and Fire might kill people, getting me involved. Shit. Darkness was all I had left and I knew that wasn't enough.

Use them all, a voice whispered in my brain. Odd. It sounded strangely like Cordelia, my friend with the psychic powers. Which was ridiculous. She was miles away, back in Portland. I had no idea if it was my brilliant mind or somebody else sending me thoughts, but it seemed as good an idea as any.

I took a deep breath and reached into the center of my being where my powers lay. I opened myself up and beckoned them, and out they came.

In a rush, all five of my abilities flew out of me, racing through my bones and across my skin. I had no idea what anyone else saw, but as my vision tunneled down into a pinprick in the Darkness, my skin glowed with fire, shimmered green with earth. The itch of my palms told me the water was ready. My hair lifted off my neck, first in a gentle breeze, then it whipped into a frenzy as the Air turned from wind to hurricane.

Opening my fists, I let the Water pour out of me. I let loose the Earth and Fire. The hurricane turned to tornado, the ground beneath my feet shook and heaved, and the air turned ice cold and burning hot, so thick with mist I could barely breathe. The tornado spun around me, a whirlwind of Water and Fire, and then I sent it outward toward the battle, whipping it around the fighters until the sound of crashing armor and swords receded, and all I could hear was the howl of the wind. All I could see was the blackness of the grave. And the Earth rushed to meet me.

# # #

It was the incessant beep that drove me from the shadowy coziness of sleep into the harsh white light of awaking. I didn't want to wake up. I wanted to stay in the quiet darkness, but the voices, the beeping, they wouldn't let me rest.

"Morgan. Morgan."

I made an unintelligible sound and batted at the annoying voice. I felt a warm trickle across my hand.

"Damn, she's pulled out the IV. Get the nurse. She's bleeding all over the place."

"Don't worry," another voice chimed in. This one soft and soothing. Calm. "We'll get her fixed up in no time."

I wanted to tell the voices to shut up. Go away and leave me alone. But I couldn't get my mouth to form the words.

"Come on, Morgan, open your eyes. Talk to me."

I finally managed to prop one eye open. I shut it again immediately as the glare singed my corneas.

"There you are." Someone was holding my hand. Skin warm against mine. Warm like the darkness where I wanted to stay. "Talk to me."

I grunted.

"Words. Use your words."

What was I? Two? I'd tell whoever it was where to stick those words. If I could get my mouth to work.

With a great deal of focus, I managed to pry my eyes open to glare at the offender. "Inigo?"

"Yeah, baby. It's me." He brushed a hand across my forehead, his blue eyes intense in a way I'd never seen them.

I tried to say, "What are you doing here?" But it came out as, "Here?"

"Yeah, I'm here."

"Water."

Someone else moved into view, handing me a pink plastic cup with a yellow straw. She held the cup while I took a couple of sips, then set it down on the table next to the bed. "How are you feeling?" She leaned over the bed, checking my IVs. She was wearing pink scrubs and her brown hair was in a short bob. She was acting terribly efficient. Nurse.

"Headache from hell," I muttered.

The nurse smiled. "That'll happen when you crack your head on a rock."

Is that what had happened? "Yeah. I guess."

"Now you lie still. I'm going to grab a doctor to check you out. Be right back." She gave Inigo a stern look. "Don't get her riled."

Inigo lifted his hands as if to protest his innocence. I couldn't help but notice the way his soft blue T-shirt pulled against well-developed muscles. Had he bulked up since the last time I saw him? Or had I just forgotten how delicious he was? Surely not. I'd need more than a bump on the head to forget that.

"Thought you were still in Scotland," I mumbled once the nurse had left.

"I was." He sank down into the chair next to my hospital bed. "But when Jack called to tell us you were in the hospital..." He shrugged as if to say it was obvious. But it wasn't. Not really. Not the way things had been between us lately.

"Us? Is Drago here?" Drago was the king of the Dragons and Inigo's half-brother.

"No. Once he sussed out what was up, he flew home."

"Why didn't he help? We could use him." A dragon to hold the line would make all the difference.

"He can't get involved. Can you imagine what would happen if the dragons got pulled into this war?"

He was right. I'd have realized it if my head didn't hurt so badly. I closed my eyes. "Thank you for coming."

"Of course I came. I love you."

17

I smiled a little at that but didn't open my eyes. "Sometimes I wonder." I wasn't sure if I'd said that out loud, or if it was my mind playing tricks on me. The darkness was pulling me down again. Into sleep. As Inigo brushed his lips against mine, I wasn't sure if it was real or if I were dreaming.

Chapter 3

I woke to find my brother, Trevor, talking in low tones with Inigo. Their faces were intense, worried.

"There you are." I turned my head, wincing slightly at the tenderness. Cordelia was sitting in a chair next to my bed, her cat, Bastet, sitting calmly in her lap. Bastet's large golden eyes blinked solemnly at me.

"Cordy. I heard you. In my head."

"Of course you did." She leaned over to pat my hand. "I thought I'd help as best I could, but when I got the call, Bastet insisted we come to the hospital immediately."

I gave Bastet a wry glance. "I'm sure she did. How did you sneak her in here? Cats aren't generally allowed in hospitals."

"There was no sneaking. The duty nurse needed a little persuading, but Bastet has her ways."

I gave the cat another sideways look. "I bet she does."

Bastet lifted her nose, all but sniffing at me. If she'd been human, I'd have taken it as a sign of her being offended.

"I assure you, she did. Bastet likes you very much." Cordy beamed at me and then at Bastet.

Cordy kept insisting her cat liked me. I'd yet to see any evidence of it. "What happened?" I asked, raising my voice so the men could hear me.

"You're awake." Trevor hurried to my bedside. "I was worried about you."

"Yeah, yeah. Hard head. What the hell happened?"

"Don't know. One minute you were standing there holding the barrier, and the next, you were on the ground bleeding. Tommy said you expended too much energy and passed out."

"I know all that," I snapped. "I mean what's got you whispering in the corner?"

Inigo and Trevor exchanged glances. Cordelia and Bastet

said nothing.

"You better tell her," Inigo said.

"Alister Jones escaped custody."

I stared at him open mouthed. Alister Jones, Kabita's father and my arch nemesis, had been "detained" at Area 51 by the SRA. It was his own fault, what with the whole killing people and trying to destroy the world thing. "Please tell me you're kidding."

"Unfortunately not."

"Christ on a bike, Trevor. What is going on over there? First Brent Darroch and now Alister. Does Kabita know?" She wouldn't be thrilled that her father was running amok.

"Yes." Trevor's tone was grim. "And there's another thing."

"Oh, lord, what now?"

"I got a call from Eddie. Alister broke in and stole the grimoire."

"Freaking fantastic." After all the trouble we'd gone to getting that thing away from him, now he had it and was on the loose. "You seriously need to think about hiring some new guards or something." My head gave a vicious throb, and I touched my forehead. Inigo came striding across the room to stand between me and my brother.

"She needs her rest," Inigo said. "You should get back to your men. Morgan might have delayed the inevitable, but the agents are the only thing holding the war back from the rest of us."

Trevor looked like he might argue. I nodded. "It's fine, Trev. I'll be fine. Go."

With a final nod, Trevor left the room. I heard him barking orders into his phone as he disappeared into the hall.

I pulled the IV out of my arm, sat up, and swung my bare legs over the edge of the bed. "Where are my clothes?"

Inigo laid a hand on my shoulder. "What are you doing? You

need to be in bed. You have a serious concussion."

"I'm fine."

"You're not. You should be dead."

"What are you talking about? I got a little bump on the head."

He gave me a look that chilled me. "Morgan, Jack told me that when he got to you, your skull was cracked open like a freaking egg."

I blinked. "No." It came out as little more than a whisper.

"Yes. The doctors said there was no way you were going to survive. As it is"—he shrugged— "thank gods you're a fast healer, but you still shouldn't be getting up." He tried to press me back down, but I resisted.

"I've got to get back to the battle and restore the barrier before it gets any worse. Then I have to go after Alister. We need to get the grimoire back. I'm fine."

He stared me straight in the eyes. "You have a headache."

How did he always know these things? I shrugged. "A little."

"Bullshit. You don't know whether to puke or pass out."

He had a point. My stomach was roiling and all I wanted to do was lay back down.

"You should do as Inigo says, Morgan," Cordy said gently. "You really aren't quite up to the task at the moment."

"We can't let Alister get away."

"We won't."

The three of us and Bastet turned toward the doorway. Kabita smiled back grimly. She looked a little worse for wear, and I was pretty sure that was demon blood streaked across her left cheek. "I've called in some backup. You, young lady, are to lie down and rest. You're not going anywhere until you can sit up without looking like you're going to pass out."

"But —"

"No buts." Inigo pressed me gently down onto the bed and

pulled the blankets up. "You heard her. It's taken care of."

"Who'd you get?" I asked reluctantly.

Kabita smiled that mysterious smile of hers. "Only the best."

"I'm the best."

She snorted. "Not right now, you're not."

"Fine. Who?"

"Haakon Magnussen. Our friendly neighborhood Viking."

"You're kidding. How'd you get him involved?" I hadn't seen Haakon since that little jaunt in the tropics. I couldn't imagine what Jack must be thinking with another Sunwalker on his turf. Still, Jack had been MIA for several weeks, and we needed help, so dude could suck it.

She shrugged. "His job was finished, and he was available. Told him we needed help and offered him a chunk of change. On the SRA's dime, of course."

"Of course." I pondered it for a moment. "No way." I sat up. "He's not going alone. I'm going with him. He doesn't know Alister like I do." I carefully avoided Kabita's gaze. We had never really talked about her father going to the dark side, so to speak, and I wasn't bringing it up until she did. It left things a little awkward sometimes.

"Morgan..." Inigo's voice held a warning.

I glanced at him. His face was expressionless, but there was that look in his eyes.

"Kabita, Cordy, can you give us a minute?"

They nodded and left the room, leaving me alone with my boyfriend for the first time in ages. And Bastet, if you could count her. But I didn't think the cat was interested in our domestic problems. "Listen to me," I said calmly, quietly. "You have no right. None. You have been absent both physically and mentally for months. I've done my best to help, and you've shut me out of your life. You have zero, and I mean zero, say in the matter."

And just like that, I realized how angry with him I was. How hurt. Betrayed. How much I wanted him to know it. Feel it. All the pain he'd caused me. I got it. I did. PTSD did stupid shit to your brain. But that didn't make it hurt any less. Or make me feel any less abandoned by the person I loved most in this world.

Because I loved him. I did. And I would do just about anything to have the man I loved back in my life. But I would not, could not, let him control me.

"Morgan, please." This time his voice was soft. His eyes were pleading. He sat beside me on the edge of the bed and took my hand in his bigger one. I felt heat rolling off him in waves. His dragon self was close to the surface, which meant his emotions were running high even if he wasn't showing it. So not like my Inigo, who'd worn his heart on his sleeve. He stroked his thumb across the back of my hand, raising shivers as he always did. "I am sorry. I can't tell you how much. I know this has been...hard. I wish it could have been different. That I could have handled it differently, but that experience—dying, being reborn—changed me."

"I know." I felt small. Sad. I wanted to curl up in a ball. But I had a job to do.

"I just want to keep you safe. We've lost so much time."

"*We* didn't lose time," I snapped. "I was here waiting for you. You were in suspended animation or whatever. You didn't suffer. I did. Then you chose to stay away, to leave me alone. The changes—those aren't the problem. That we could have dealt with. But you shut me out."

He nodded. "I needed my space. I won't apologize for that. But I will apologize for hurting you in the process, because that is something I never want to do."

"Too late."

He nodded, and this time I saw the bone-deep sadness in

him. "I know. And I will spend as long as it takes making it up to you."

"By bossing me around?" I quirked an eyebrow, or tried. They both went up. Damn eyebrows.

The slightest smile played about his lips. "You know me. Can't help myself. Sometimes you drive me nuts."

And then I was laughing, which made my head hurt like hell. But I didn't care because for the first time in a very long time, Inigo was laughing too.

Chapter 4

Inigo talked me into staying in the hospital at least until Haakon touched down. I agreed, if only to shut him up. And also because my head still hurt. Plus the nurse kind of scared me, although she didn't complain when Bastet climbed onto the foot of my bed and curled up. You'd think that was a sweet gesture, but you'd be wrong. The cat used every opportunity to shoot me a nasty glare.

Cordelia had hauled Inigo to the other side of the room in order to read his cards. He'd been reluctant, but I was relieved. Right now I just wanted a little peace and quiet.

I tried to use the time to think things through about Inigo and me, but eventually I gave up. The headache was too much, and frankly, I didn't want to think anymore. I'd rather just feel, and what I was feeling was hope. Hope that things between us would finally be okay again.

With three hours before Haakon was due to arrive, my cell phone rang. I frowned when I saw Trevor's name on my screen.

"Morgan, we need you. Now."

"What happened?"

"The dome is down."

"The whole thing?"

"Yes." His tone was terse. "Get here." He hung up.

I swung my legs out of bed. "Where are my clothes?" Bastet jumped off the bed with a sniff and joined Cordelia near the window.

"No, wait. You promised." Inigo tried to press me back down on the bed, but I swatted his hand away. "You need rest."

"The dome is down. I have to fix it or resting will be the least of my worries. Now, clothes." I snapped my fingers.

Inigo rolled his eyes but brought me my clothes. Cordy looked amused.

"Why do you have to go fix it?" Inigo asked. "Isn't that what put you in the hospital in the first place?"

I shimmied into my jeans. "Overdoing it put me in the hospital. I channeled too much at once. I won't do it again."

"And how are you going to avoid it?"

"I'll think of something," I said testily.

"Ice."

Both of us turned to stare at Cordelia. I yanked my T-shirt over my head. "Ice?"

She gave me an angelic smile. Oh, lord, she was away with the fairies again. "Yes. It came to me."

The voices. Goody. "Could you be more specific?" I sat down on the bed to pull on my socks and boots.

"That's all they gave me." She sighed as she stroked Bastet's back. The cat let out a contented purr. See, that was what cats did when they liked you.

"Okay, then." I snagged my jacket off the chair and shrugged into it. "I guess I'll see what I can do. Weapons?"

"In your car," Inigo said. "Down in the parking lot. Jack put them in the trunk. He didn't think the hospital would appreciate them in your room."

"Good point." I turned to Cordy. "You coming?"

"What would I do that for? I don't have the necessary magic." She placed Bastet gently on the floor and stood, shaking out her robe. "Now that you're all right, Bastet and I will head home. Until you need us." She strode out, Bastet trotting along behind her.

I shook my head. "Let's go."

The sun was setting when we left the car at Tommy's cabin and hiked across the high desert toward the battle. I heard the clash of weaponry and the explosions of magic long before the war zone came into sight. I winced when I saw the scorched earth. It looked even worse than it had earlier, and Trevor was right: the barrier was down completely.

Tommy waved us over toward a cluster of sagebrush a safe distance from the battle. Safe being a relative term. I could see Trevor's SRA agents ranged around the battlefield, weapons in their hands. They were different from the ones I'd seen earlier. Definitely not your standard automatic rifles.

"Tesselah stopped by earlier," Tommy said with a nod toward the agents. "She worked up something new for the boys to try out. Seems to be working so far."

Tesselah was a genius with weaponry effective against supernatural elements. I'd had the pleasure of using many of her experimental gadgets over the years.

"What are they?"

He pursed his lips. "Temporal guns."

"Temporal guns. Really."

"Well, there were a few other words involved. It was a very long title."

"What do they do?"

"Act as a temporary barrier. The fighters get too near the line, the agent shoots them and up goes a momentary barrier preventing them from getting any closer. It's a stop gap, nothing more."

"Can we reactivate the barrier?" Inigo asked.

"Permanently, no. We need a witch for that, and since Kabita set it, she's got to fix it."

"Did you call her?" I asked.

"She's a little busy at the moment. Apparently the demon infestation turned out to be a little bigger than she thought."

I gave him a look. "Bigger?"

"The pastor was the one who summoned them."

"Holy shit." Inigo's eyes were wide.

"You aren't kidding. We must do this ourselves."

"How?" I didn't think I could reactivate the dome. I didn't have that kind of ability.

"I believe I can raise the barrier again, at least temporarily. If we can figure out a way to keep it in place…"

"Ice!"

Both men turned to stare at me.

"Cordy said I should use ice, remember?" I turned to Inigo.

He nodded. "Yeah, but you didn't know what that meant."

"I do now. Tommy, if you raise the barrier, I can coat it with Ice."

"It's a little warm for that," Tommy pointed out.

"Sure. If it were normal ice. But it isn't. I'll put it on good and thick. It ought to hold for a while. Long enough for me to go after Alister, anyway."

"Why didn't you do this before?" Tommy asked.

"Hadn't thought of it." And I probably still wouldn't have if Cordelia hadn't pointed it out.

He nodded. "All right then. Let's try it."

We followed him to the nearest ward. He knelt down and placed his hands around it and began to chant in a low voice, rocking back and forth with the rhythm. While he did that I called Trevor.

"Pull your men back. We're going to raise the barrier."

"Got it."

I watched as the agents began to fall back, away from the fighting. They kept their guns raised, pointed at the combatants.

Tommy's chanting grew more intense. Then the dome began to shimmer. Well, more like sputter. It flashed and sparked as if it were trying to restore itself but didn't have quite enough juice.

"That's the best I can do," Tommy muttered, voice strained. "Get to it."

I nodded. Reaching inside me, I grabbed hold of the sparkling blue I knew was Water. I pulled it toward me, demanding its cooperation. It was reluctant at first, but then it flowed toward me in undulating waves until it burst out through the center of my chest.

Focusing, I sent it toward the dome. It splashed against the nearly invisible walls, coating the entire dome in Water. Then with a thought, I froze the water solid. It formed a thin crust of ice around the dome.

"That's not enough," Inigo murmured. "They'll break through that in seconds."

If it were real ice. But it wasn't. Still, he was right. I needed more.

I sent another wave washing across the dome, and then another. I froze each layer until I had a thick rime of ice built up. I took a deep breath and pushed the Water back inside. It went with surprising ease. Apparently it was as tired as I was.

Inside, somebody rammed the wall of the dome. We all held our breath, waiting for cracks. When none showed, we breathed a sigh of relief.

"How long will it hold?" Inigo asked.

"No idea," I admitted. "Trevor's agents will have to stay here and keep an eye on it."

"As will I," Tommy said.

"You don't need to." I reached out to grasp his arm. "You've done enough already."

He patted my hand. "Until my people are safe, my duty is not done. Go. Find Alister Jones. Save the world."

I snorted. "Melodramatic much?" He gave me a smile that reminded me of Cordelia's and turned to watch the dome.

###

Inigo had insisted on driving to the airport and I let him. My head still hurt, and while I'd taken the lowest dose of painkillers possible, it was still making me a little lightheaded. Probably the whole water channeling thing hadn't helped.

Haakon was already waiting for us on the sidewalk outside "Arrivals" as Inigo pulled my Mustang into PDX, Portland International Airport. I'd forgotten how big Haakon was. His massive frame loomed above the rest of the crowd, his blond hair shining in the late afternoon sun. He wore a black biker jacket, well-worn jeans that hugged his massive thighs, and he carried what looked like a black ops duffel. It was as if a Viking had woken up one day in the modern era, which wasn't far off the mark, believe it or not. Haakon, like Jack, was a Sunwalker. Only he was a couple hundred years older than Jack.

We pulled up to the curb, I climbed out and flipped the seat forward. He gave me a look that said "Seriously?" before he practically launched himself into the backseat. I caught several females appreciating his backside.

"Problem?" I asked sweetly.

He glared at me. "I'd rather face a passel of Hel cats," he muttered, turning to share his ire with the still ogling women while I strapped myself back in.

I couldn't help a small giggle. "Haakon, this is my—" What was Inigo? Was he still my boyfriend? He was finally beginning to act like it again. "—boyfriend, Inigo."

"Nice to meet you," Inigo said, glancing in the rearview mirror as he pulled out.

Haakon stared at the back of Inigo's head. "Dragon."

Startled, I whipped around. "What?"

He tilted his head as if listening for something. "Surely you know your boyfriend is a dragon."

"Of course I do. But how did you know?"

He smiled slyly. "I have my ways." He threw a glance at

Inigo. "Nice to meet you. Been a while since I worked with dragonkin."

"Your neck of the woods is a little colder than we like."

Haakon grunted in agreement. "Too cold for my liking sometimes."

"Kabita told you what's going on?" I asked.

"She did."

"How did she convince you?"

He gave me a look. "I was bored."

Fantastic. A bored Viking Sunwalker. Just what I needed. "Maybe you should help Jack and the SRA," I suggested. "They could use some muscle."

Haakon snorted. "Not a chance. I'm a Hunter." He eyed me. "Like you. I've never been a solider."

"I don't know. Viking warrior sounds pretty badass."

He lifted a blond brow. "What makes you think I went *aviking*?"

"Didn't you?"

He didn't answer. Great. Another Tall, Blond, and Silent. Just what I needed. "Fine. Let's talk Alister. It's not going to be easy finding him."

"Dude's a slippery eel," Haakon agreed.

Inigo seemed to find that amusing. I shook my head. "Right. So, we need a plan."

Haakon studied me. "I assume you have one in mind."

"Of course. We start with where he escaped."

"Doesn't your brother already know how he escaped?"

"Sure. But I like to look at things with my own eyes."

He grunted. "Waste of time. You've got a trained agent at your disposal. You don't need to go sticking your nose in where a job's already been done."

I bristled at that, but Inigo laid a warm hand on my thigh. "He's right. Talk to Trevor. Get the details. We'll go from there."

"In the meantime, I'm starving. I could use a burger." Haakon leaned back in his seat appearing calm and collected, but his eyes danced like a little boy's at the circus.

"You want burgers. You got burgers." Inigo grinned widely, and suddenly I was hit by the likeness to his old self.

"Yeah," I whispered, my heart aching. "I could go for a burger."

Chapter 5

While Haakon and Inigo went into Burgerville to get our food, I stayed in the car and FaceTimed my brother. Trevor answered. Even though it was almost full dark, I could tell he was looking haggard, dark smudges beneath his eyes and his face sweaty and streaked with soot.

"How's it going?" I asked.

He gave me a look. "Seriously?"

"That bad, huh?"

"Not good. But we're holding."

"The dome?"

"Your ice fortress? Still up."

"Good." If they could hold long enough, maybe this thing would burn itself out. Then again, that was probably wishful thinking. The Queen of the Sidhe had been planning this for a long time. I just wasn't sure yet what her endgame was. "Listen, I need details on Alister's escape. What do you know?"

He ducked as an explosion rocked the ground nearby. I heard somebody shouting in the background. It sounded like Jack. "Not much," he admitted. "The guys at Area 51 contacted me early this morning. The guard went to deliver his breakfast as usual, and the cage was empty. Alister was gone. No sign of how he did it. The door hadn't been opened, no one appeared on camera, no burn marks like with Darroch. Just gone."

"When was the last time anyone saw him?"

"In person? When the guard delivered dinner last night about six o'clock."

"And nobody noticed he was gone until this morning?"

Another explosion sent bits of dirt flying through the air. Trevor grimaced and brushed dirt out of his hair.

"I thought you said the dome was still up," I snapped.

"It is, but the magic fireball whatsits are still getting through

33

from time to time."

"Damn."

"Yeah. Anyway. The guards don't enter the area where Alister was kept except during meal times. The rest of the time, the prisoners are on camera constantly. There are guards watching nonstop on screens in another location. Alister was on-screen the entire time."

"How exactly?"

"What do you mean?"

"What did he do while he was on-screen?"

He stared at me for a moment. "What are you thinking?"

"Just tell me."

He huffed, glancing toward what I guess was the action. "Okay, quickly. Alister ate his dinner and put his tray in the slot about forty-five minutes later. Then he cleaned up. By seven he was in bed reading. Nine o'clock was lights out; that's when the cameras switch to infra-red. Alister was in bed the entire time."

"It was the switch."

"Excuse me?"

"There's a hitch between when the cameras switch from regular to infra, right?"

He nodded slowly. "Shit. You think that's when they switched the feed?"

"Has to be."

"But the video wasn't tampered with."

"The video, no. I bet it was the feed itself. Your cameras thought they were seeing Alister in bed, but he was in fact escaping."

"I don't see how."

I did. "There's only one way. The Fairy Queen opened a portal into his cage and let him through to the Otherworld."

"But why would she do that? She and Alister aren't exactly friends."

It was true. Darroch had been her ally, not Alister. "Things change."

"What are you going to do?"

I smiled grimly. "Find a way into Faerie."

Haakon and Inigo seemed to be taking an inordinate amount of time getting burgers. I decided to join them. Maybe that would hurry things up, or at least keep me from twiddling my thumbs in boredom.

Pushing open the door, I stepped out of the Mustang. I didn't even have time to shut the door before something grabbed me.

Without thinking I lashed out, sinking an elbow into my attacker. Whoever it was let out an *oomph*, but didn't let go of me. A tight grip on the back of my skull told me what he was: vampire.

How had I not noticed before? My head gave a throb to remind me. Oh, yeah. Headache. Plus I'd been worried about the whole djinn/Sidhe war thing.

My sword and machete were in the trunk. The only weapons I was carrying were a gun with lead bullets meant for the Sidhe, which would be less than useless, and a small Sidhe-crafted blade. Not exactly vampire fighting material.

I kicked back, connecting with a knee. This time there was a howl, and the grip loosened enough so I could twist out of the vamp's grasp. Dropping to one knee, I slipped the blade from my boot.

The vampire attacked again, and I sank the blade hilt-deep in its chest. It snarled as thick, dark blood pooled around its chest. Dammit. Too far to the right. I'd missed its heart.

It grabbed me, yanking me close. Its eyes glowed faintly red in the dark: one of Alister's soul vampires. Except this one didn't really seem very aware. More like feral. Either it was an experiment gone wrong, or whatever Alister had done to it was wearing off.

It opened its mouth wide, clearly expecting to sink its fangs into my throat. Instead I slapped my palm against its chest and summoned the Fire. With a shriek of delight, it burst out of me, engulfing the vampire in roaring flames.

I stumbled back, watching the vamp burn. It howled in pain and then burst into dust. The flame disappeared, and the Fire sank back inside me without me even trying.

I suddenly noticed a woman sitting in a car a few spots down staring at me with wide eyes. She had plastic curlers on her head and was clearly in her pajamas. Late evening snack, I guessed.

I waved at her. "Don't worry," I called. "He's okay. Just a trial run for the TV show. You know, gotta practice the stunts."

She didn't look convinced. "You're from that series? The one with the were-animals?"

"Yep." I gave her an innocent grin. The TV show, filmed in Portland, was super popular. It was the best cover story I could come up with under the circumstances.

"Okay." She still looked freaked out. She revved her engine and practically peeled out of the parking lot.

"Morgan!"

I glanced up to see Inigo and Haakon jogging toward me. They weren't carrying any food.

"Are you all right? What happened?" Inigo stared down at the pile of dust.

I stooped to pick up my blade. "Vamp attack. No big thing."

Haakon raised a blond brow. "Here? In the middle of a public parking lot?"

"Yeah. One of Alister's minions. It looked like he was a little crazed. More than usual for a vamp, anyway. It's fine. He's dead.

I'm not."

"I wish you'd take these things more seriously," Inigo muttered.

"What I take seriously is a lack of food. I'm hungry."

With a sigh, Inigo jogged back to collect the forgotten food. Haakon remained, his hand hovering near his belt where I knew he kept at least one blade, maybe more.

"You sure you're okay?"

"Fine."

"This could be Alister coming after you."

I shook my head, wincing a little at the residual headache. "I don't think so. Pretty sure this guy was at the end of whatever control Alister had over him. Random thing, probably."

"More likely he was following the orders Alister gave him when he first imbued his soul."

I shrugged. "I guess."

Inigo returned with the burgers, and we all climbed into the car and dug in with gusto. While we ate, I told them about my chat with Trevor and my suspicions about Alister's location, as well as my determination to follow him to the Otherworld.

"But the Queen is the only one who can open a portal," Inigo said. Haakon sat in the backseat and munched on his fries, ignoring the byplay between us. Smart man.

"That's true," I admitted. "At least it used to be. Maybe there's another way."

"What are you talking about?"

I sighed. "You've been gone awhile."

His expression hardened. "That wasn't my fault."

"True, but it was partially your choice. A lot of things happened while you were away."

I saw the dread in his eyes. Was he afraid I'd cheated on him or something? Shit.

"My powers, okay? They've grown."

I think he was relieved, but it was hard to tell. "Tell me."

"Apparently, in addition to Darkness, Fire and Air, I can now channel Earth and Water."

"What does that mean exactly?"

"I get to do groovy things like shoot icicles out of my palms."

"You're kidding."

"She's not," Haakon spoke from the backseat. Inigo turned to stare at him, but Haakon munched contentedly on his burger, not offering any more information. Inigo looked like he was about to start smoking from the ears. Not a good thing for a dragon. Next he'd be breathing fire, and my beloved Mustang would be a hulk of smoking metal.

"Back when you were still in, uh, recovery in that egg thing, Jack and I were running around Paris after Alister."

"You went to Paris with Jack?"

I eyed him. "Are you jealous?"

He thought it over, then gave me a long, slow, sexy smile. "Not even a little. But I promise you, you and me are going to Paris one day."

I grinned. "Anyway, we ended up chasing Darroch into the Otherworld. I'd just started channeling Earth, so things were a little fritzy, but the next thing I knew, I was controlling a damn fairy."

Inigo's eyes widened. "How?"

"No idea. When I used my powers around the Marid, he was able to control them and me. I figured Morgana and her minions would be the same, but apparently not. When I use Earth power, I can control the fae. At least a little bit."

"And how is that going to help us?"

"Well," I said, tapping my thumb on the dashboard. "I'm hoping it will help me open a portal. But I'm going to need a witch."

"Call Kabita."

"I need somebody stronger. Somebody with a very particular set of abilities."

Haakon glanced up then, his face expressionless. Our eyes met in the rearview mirror. Some sort of vibe passed between us, I just wasn't sure what.

"I take it you know the right person," Inigo said dryly.

"I do."

"Well, then." He strapped on his seatbelt and turned the key. "What are we waiting for?"

#

Emory Chastain's shop was in a cute little vintage storefront wedged between an antique store whose owners had a fondness for teacups and an empty building with Coming Soon plastered across the plate glass window. The shop had been left to her by her aunt, along with the old crumbling Victorian she lived in, which was why Emory had moved to Portland in the first place. She was a friend of Eddie's, and she'd helped us with our little problem aboard the steampunk cruise. Although she'd been hesitant when I called, she'd agreed to try and open a portal to the Otherworld.

I pushed the door open. Instead of the usual bell or annoying electronic chime, there was a small wind chime which tinkled as I walked beneath it. I found it charming.

The air was redolent with the scent of dried herbs and essential oils. One wall was lined with glass shelves, each stocked with bars of soap and interestingly shaped bottles of who knew what. An antique apothecary chest sat against another wall, the top crammed with clear glass jars filled with dried herbs. Each little drawer was clearly labeled, although unreadable from my vantage point across the room. Wobbly vintage tables with shabby chic paint jobs dotted the room and were stacked with books on herbs, beeswax candles in various colors, and brightly colored tins.

A large crystal chandelier, suspended from the ceiling in the center of the room, cast rainbows across the wide plank floors. The long, marble-topped cashier desk looked like something out of the 1800s, its mahogany base dented and scratched by a thousand booted feet and wayward umbrellas. More dried herbs hung from the exposed beams and little brown tincture bottles filled shelves behind the register.

Emory turned from where she'd been reorganizing one of the tables. She was wearing a scarlet broomstick skirt—hadn't those gone out of fashion in the 90s?—paired with a loose, white peasant shirt trimmed in colorful embroidery. Her feet were bare, as usual, her toes painted an eye-popping stripper pink. Her strawberry blonde hair tumbled down her back in curls and waves finishing off the wild, bohemian look. I was never sure if it was a put-on or just who she was.

"Morgan." She gave me a tight smile but otherwise appeared as tranquil as ever.

"Thanks for agreeing to help," I said, walking toward her.

"Don't thank me yet. I'm not even sure this will work." She glanced behind me. "Mr. Magnussen. Nice to see you again." She sounded like she meant it, but it was hard to tell.

Haakon gave her a gracious nod. "Ms. Chastain."

"And who is your friend?" Emory turned toward Inigo, who thrust out his hand.

"Inigo Jones." He glanced at me. "Morgan's boyfriend."

My heart gave a little flutter. So he still wanted to be claimed as belonging to me. Or maybe it was me belonging to him. Part of me was relieved but another part was still irked he seemed to think it would be so easy to go back to the way things were.

Things could never be the way they were.

I shook off my maudlin thoughts. I needed to focus. We needed to find Alister and stop him before it was too late to deal with whatever nastiness he had up his sleeve.

"What do we do?" I asked Emory.

"Give me a moment." She strode to the front of the store, flipped the sign to Closed, and turned the deadbolt. Then she returned to us, her long skirt swishing around her ankles. "Follow me."

She led us into a back room and turned on the overhead lights. In the glare of the fluorescents, I saw it was not unlike Eddie's storage room at Majicks and Potions, except it was a lot neater. Two rows of shelving units, three units deep, lined either side of a center aisle. Emory walked to the back of the room before slipping out of sight behind the final row of shelving. I hurried after her to find she'd vanished. The only hint to her location was the flutter of a midnight blue velvet curtain blocking a narrow doorway cut into the sheetrock. I followed her.

Beyond the curtain was a much smaller room. The walls were painted deep purple, the ceiling and floor black. A simple Wiccan shrine was tucked into a small alcove on the wall opposite the doorway. A metal and glass curio cabinet stood next to it. The middle of the floor was completely bare.

"Stand against the wall until I'm finished," Emory ordered. I moved, waving the guys over as they entered. She opened the curio cabinet and took out something. I couldn't tell what it was until she turned, knelt down on the floor, and began drawing an intricate design. Chalk.

Emory drew several symbols in a wide circle. The symbols looked familiar, not unlike Atlantean. I opened my mouth to question her but thought better of it. I didn't need to distract the woman who was about to open a portal to the Otherworld. Good way to end up on the hell planes. Not my idea of fun.

Within the circle of symbols, Emory sketched another, this one larger and far more intricate. It looked somewhat like a labyrinth but with a lot more swirls. I'd never seen anything like it. She returned the chalk to the curio cabinet and returned carrying several white candles. She placed one on each of the outer symbols, plus a single one in the very center of the circle. Another trip to the cabinet produced a clay jar, which she opened, pouring the contents on the floor in a wide circle around the symbols. Salt.

Placing the jar on the floor next to the circle, she eyed us sternly. "Whatever happens, do not cross the salt line until I tell you. Got it?"

We nodded obediently. I guessed she was fine with our answer because she moved toward the center candle. Closing her eyes and holding her hands above it, she began to chant. The candle sparked, and then the wick flamed. Emory faced each of the four corners in turn, and while I couldn't understand her words, I knew she was invoking the elements. The powers inside me stirred restlessly. I tamped down harder on the metaphorical lid between them and the outside world.

Once the elements were called, Emory slowly walked the circle, her athame tracing each symbol. As she passed each candle, its wick burst into flame. I swayed to the rhythm of her chant, the powers inside me straining to get out, wanting the warmth of the circle and the energy that lived there. Inigo grabbed my arm, and I realized I'd taken a step forward. I nodded in thanks, and he removed his hand. Haakon never took his eyes off Emory.

I felt the moment the circle slammed shut. The final candle lit, and there was an invisible rush of...something. I couldn't see it, but the powers in me stilled, no longer called by whatever the hell was inside with Emory.

Returning to the center flame, Emory once again held her

hands above it, chanting. The flames leapt higher as her chanting intensified. Then she pulled a small vial from between her breasts. I hadn't even seen her put it there. Still chanting she uncorked the tiny bottle, waving her palm above it in a circle. Then she swallowed the contents in one gulp. Tucking the empty vial away, she continued chanting.

The air around the circle began to spark and sizzle like a downed electrical cable in a storm. Except there was no cable, and there was no storm. Colors rolled across the barrier in shimmers like the Aurora Borealis. Pinks, blues, and finally greens. Every green you could imagine from the palest celery to the deepest forest and everything in between. Golden sparkles drifted across the colors and away from the edge into the center of the circle, coalescing into a shimmering orb above Emory's outstretched hands.

Golden light from the orb bathed her face, highlighting her high cheekbones and casting her eyes into dark shadows. The sparkles flew faster, turning into streaks of light slamming into the orb as it grew larger and larger.

Something shifted in the room. Like pressure before a thunderstorm. Or your ears after takeoff when all they needed to do was pop.

Everything went still, and I realized Emory had finally stopped chanting. She was staring at the orb swirling above her hands. It was now the size of a basketball, pulsing like a heart.

"Oh, crap..." I whispered.

The orb exploded.

Chapter 6

I ducked instinctively, convinced the entire room was about to disintegrate around us. Inigo threw himself over me as if he could protect me from the blast. His skin shimmered into blue scales as he half morphed into his dragon form. Maybe he could protect me at that.

As we crouched there, I realized the explosion had had no sound. The room was quiet. Nothing was out of place. The walls were intact, the floor still under our feet. Well, knees in this case. I peeked out from underneath Inigo's protective arms and saw the circle was untouched, the colors calmly swirling across its surface like wind over lake water on a summer's day.

"Off me," I grunted, pushing at Inigo. He didn't budge

"The explosion..."

"We're fine. Nothing happened out here." I pushed at him again. This time he let me up.

"What the Hades?"

"That's what I want to know," I said grimly, walking toward the circle. Haakon was already there, trying to peer through the opaque colors blocking our view.

"We should go in," Haakon said grimly. He was braced as if ready to throw himself bodily through the barrier.

"No we shouldn't. She told us not to cross the circle until she told us to. Believe me, magic is not something you want to mess with."

"You know very well there is no such thing as magic." His tone was haughty, which was pretty funny seeing as how he'd probably believed very firmly in magic a thousand years ago.

"Yeah, yeah. Quantum physics yada yada. It's easier to just call it magic. All right?" Trying to wrap my head around science as wild as what Emory had dipped into was enough to give me a migraine. Humans had been calling this stuff "magic" for millennia. Who was I to change things? "We stay out of the circle."

The colors slowly began to turn translucent, fading and drifting away into whatever ether from which they'd come. I could see glimpses inside the circle. The explosion had knocked over the candles and, thank goodness, extinguished the flames. It had even scorched the floor, smudging the chalk figures. But the circle held, which meant Emory was alive.

And then I saw it. Shimmering in the center about two feet off the ground was a portal. Like an oval mirror suspended in the air, its surface shimmering slightly. Below the mirror huddled a figure, still as death.

"Emory. Emory, are you okay?"

Without a word, Haakon stormed toward the circle. I grabbed him by the arm, but he was too strong for even my Hunter strength. "Inigo!"

But I needn't have shouted. Inigo was there, physically blocking Haakon from entering the circle. Dragon versus Sunwalker was a little more of an even match.

"Chill, buddy," Inigo said in that old, charming tone he used to use so often. My heart shuddered. It felt like ages since I'd heard it. "Emory told us what to do. We do it. If she wanted us to rescue her, she would have told us beforehand."

"She could not have known this would happen." Haakon's voice was a snarl. He shoved at Inigo.

"Maybe she did. Maybe she didn't." Inigo didn't move an inch. "But she's Witch Blood. She told us what to do, and we need to do it. No telling what will happen if we breach that circle."

"She could be injured."

I glanced at Emory's inert body. "She could be," I admitted. "But it doesn't matter. We stay on this side of the circle until she calls us. Believe me. You do not want to mess with Witch magic.

45

If it doesn't kill you, she will."

"I told you it isn't magic."

"All the more reason not to mess with it. Do you make a habit of arguing with gravity?"

He clenched his jaw.

"Didn't think so. Now do what Inigo said and chill. You're no good to us going off halfcocked."

Haakon raised his brow but backed down. "I am a Viking. Sitting still is not in our nature."

"I'm a Hunter. It's not in mine, either. Guess what? We both get to put on our Big Girl Panties."

Inigo smirked. Haakon stared at me.

Emory chose that moment to roll over and glare at us. "Would you all stop yammering and get in here and help me?"

Haakon practically shoved me out of the way in his hurry to get to Emory. He knelt and gently helped her to her feet. Did Haakon have a crush on Emory? I watched them closely. Haakon was definitely hovering in an overly concerned way but not really in an "I want to see you naked way." More like an "I've sworn an oath of protection" way. Shit. Not another Jack.

I stepped into the circle, feeling a slight zing along my skin as I passed through. Inside, I heard the hum of the portal and smelled the ozone burn mixed with lush, green things. The portal definitely led to the Otherworld. Inigo joined us, and the space in front of the portal seemed to shrink.

"How long do you plan to be gone?" Emory asked.

I shrugged. "Long as it takes. I have no idea where Alister is, but we have to find him."

"I can't maintain the circle indefinitely."

"Aren't you coming with us?" Haakon asked.

She gave him a look. "I'm a Witch. No way I'm getting caught in the Otherworld."

I had no idea what terrible things would befall Witches who

wandered into Morgana's territory, but clearly Emory did. By the look on her face, it wasn't anything good. "How do we get back?"

"I'll keep the portal open as long as I can."

"Can't you just open it again?" Inigo asked.

"I can," Emory admitted. "But who knows where it will lead. Or when. And every time I use my magic to open a portal, I leave a sign for the Queen to follow. I will not have her follow me here, understand?"

"We understand," I assured her. "Just keep it open as long as possible." I didn't mention I might be able to open a portal from the Otherworld. I'd never actually done it before, though I had controlled one, and no telling if I could do it or not. The last thing I wanted was to get stuck in Morgana's territory.

Emory checked her watch, humming slightly to herself. "Make it fast. I can hold this thing open only so long. If you're not back when it closes, you're on your own."

Chapter 7

I tumbled out of the portal and hit the ground rolling. I lay panting on the grass, ignoring the sword sheath poking into my spine, until Inigo tumbled out after me. I rolled out of the way so he wouldn't crush me and staggered to my feet. The land of the Sidhe looked exactly as it had every other time I'd been here. Green, green everywhere. Even the air smelled green.

The portal opened onto a small clearing not far from a stream. I heard the sound of rushing water not far away. On every side we were surrounded by the dense forest of the Otherworld, which was filled with semi-sentient trees and flora with a hunger for human flesh. It was no wonder that people who wandered through the Queen's portal by accident rarely returned to our world. And here I was popping in and out like a prodigal daughter.

Was it me, or were the woods a little more ominous than before? The tree trunks seemed closer together and darker somehow. The underbrush was definitely heavier, and it rustled liked creatures were watching us. Since it was the Otherworld, I was nearly certain it was the bushes themselves doing the watching. I repressed a shudder.

Inigo hauled himself to his feet and glanced around in awe. This was his first time to fairyland.

"Holy shit, there's a lot of green." He sniffed. "I don't like the smell of the place."

I inhaled again. "All I smell is green stuff."

He shook his head. "Underneath there's something..." He sniffed again. "It smells foul. Like something's dead."

I couldn't smell it, but the whole half-dragon thing gave him a definite advantage in that department. I'd have to take his word for it. Just then, Haakon tumbled out of the portal. He lay flat on his back in the grass, staring up at the green-tinged sky.

"What a rush." He sat up, blinking his ice blue eyes. "Although I could have done without the landing." He rubbed the back of his head and staggered to his feet, adjusting his weaponry. "Where to?"

"The last time I was here, Morgana had a castle somewhere nearby. I imagine Alister will be there."

"How can you tell it was around here?" Haakon asked. "Everything looks the same."

"That's what you think," I mumbled. I glanced around, taking in my surroundings. I was fairly certain we weren't far from the clearing where the Queen's portal had spat us out on my last trip, but this place was entirely unfamiliar. The guys were staring at me, waiting for me to make the next move. Crap. What now?

Last time I was in the Otherworld, I'd been able to control one of the lesser fae. A tiny winged creature. It hadn't been happy, but it had done what I told it. Maybe I could call one of those things, whatever they were, and make it show us the way. Maybe it could even tell us where Alister was for certain.

"All right, stay back," I said. "I'm going to call a Sidhe."

The two men exchanged glances but otherwise said nothing. I guessed they were used to my powers by now. Good for them. I sure wasn't.

Taking a deep breath, I closed my eyes and mentally reached into the center of my being where my powers slept fitfully. Eager at my approach, they roiled around each other, trying to get out. I forced them back, allowing only Earth to answer my call. It slid slowly out of its hiding spot, unfurling through my body like a living thing. Twining down my arms in shimmering vines of verdant green, it wrapped itself around me like a lover.

I visualized it forcing its way into the ground beneath our feet. The earth began to shake. Haakon and Inigo staggered a little as the ground gave a solid heave. My feet remained rooted, held in place by my power. I willed it out into the Otherworld, searching, seeking, until it found what I needed: a tiny speck of sentient life in all the wild green.

Not that the plants of the Otherworld weren't sentient. They were, after a fashion, but this spot of color was different. *Come to me*, I ordered. The tiny being resisted, but not for long. With reluctance it began to move my way.

"It's coming," I said.

"What is?" Haakon asked suspiciously.

I didn't answer. It was already here. A tiny winged creature flitted into the clearing. It was about the size of a tiger swallowtail butterfly, only its wings were pale lavender spotted with lemon yellow. It sparkled beneath the green sun like it had been attacked by glitter.

"What do you want?" it snapped sharply in its small, squeaky voice. I heard the unsaid "bitch" in its tone.

"Alister Jones," I said. "You know who he is?"

The tiny creature sighed and crossed its arms, beating its wings furiously to keep aloft. "Who's asking?"

I sent out a tendril of my power and wrapped it tight around the little bug. "You know who I am."

It snarled, flashing wickedly sharp teeth at me. "I know. Hunter."

"Then tell me what I wish to know."

"Fine," it snapped. "Yeah, Jones is here. Whining pain in the ass. Thinks he's king of the damn universe."

"The Queen is hiding him?"

"Shhhh." It looked like it might rupture a spleen. "Don't say her name. Do you want her to hear us?" The creature glanced around, terrified, as if the bushes were full of the Queen's men. Which they might be, though I doubted it. My Earth power would have sensed them.

"Is she? Hiding Alister Jones?"

"Of course she is."

"Why?"

"How the Titania should I know?" Apparently using the names of dead Sidhe queens was acceptable. "She doesn't answer to the likes of me."

"But you know where Alister Jones is."

It shrugged. "Of course. All of Fairy knows where she stashed him. In that damn castle of hers."

"Show me."

It sighed. "Fine. Whatever. If I do, will you leave me alone?"

"Once you show me the way, I will let you go."

"This way." It flitted off into the trees, and I followed. Haakon seemed doubtful, but Inigo didn't hesitate, tromping along behind me. Eventually Haakon came along, grumbling. For a Viking, he could sure be whiny.

I followed the winged fae for what seemed like hours but it was probably only about fifteen minutes until we burst out of the overgrown woodland into what passed for sun in the Otherworld. We were in a small clearing at the edge of a cliff. Far below that cliff rushed the black, ominous waters of a raging river.

"That path leads to the castle," the little creature said, pointing to a narrow track barely visible between two enormous trees. "I think you can make it on your own from here. Unless you're too stupid." It sneered at me. "Now let me go."

"Fine. Go." I released my power from it but gave it a good swat with my hand for the "stupid" remark. It squealed angrily as it tumbled through the air and tangled in the branches of a tree. I could still hear its tiny voice cussing me out in two different languages as the three of us headed down the trail.

"Looks like a goat trail." Haakon stared at the path leading to the castle. His mood wasn't improving.

"Don't be an ass," I snapped. His eyes widened. "It's the

same trail Jack and I took from the castle when we were chasing Brent Darroch. If he can manage it, so can you."

"What is it with this guy and the Sidhe Queen?" Inigo wondered aloud. Nobody answered. It was rhetorical. We had no idea what Alister and Morgana were up to, but it couldn't be good.

As we followed the path toward the castle, the air became increasingly thick until it was like breathing soup. It was hot, too. Hotter than the bloody jungle we'd tromped through in the Caribbean. Trailing vines slapped at bare arms and faces, and heavy branches dripped water on us until our clothes were soaked. It must have rained recently.

It seemed like ages before we finally escaped the forest onto the hillside overlooking the Queen's castle. Had the black stone grown darker since the last time I'd seen it?

"There's no way we can make it back to the portal quickly," Inigo murmured. "It's been ten minutes already, and we're not even to the castle yet."

Only ten minutes? Guess time really did pass differently in the Otherworld. I smiled grimly. "Don't worry. I've got a plan."

"Sure hope so," Haakon muttered. "This place is too hot for my blood."

I ignored him. "Let's go."

It took another ten minutes to reach the bridge that spanned the river in front of the castle. Distances, like time, were deceiving in the Otherworld. The gate stood wide open, allowing easy access to the castle courtyard. As we pressed closer to the portico, I saw something dripping down the castle walls. Thick, black sludge oozed across the black stones. No wonder it looked darker. I sniffed and almost gagged. It smelled worse, too.

"I don't like this," Haakon growled, sliding his sword from the sheath along his back. Not that it would do him any good.

The Sidhe were impervious to man-made weapons. Only a Sidhe blade could kill a Sidhe.

"I don't like it, either," Inigo said, his voice low. "I know the Queen's Guard is off fighting the djinn, but this doesn't feel right. There should still be guards."

I agreed, but we didn't have a lot of options. "Fan out," I said. "The faster we find Alister, the faster we can get the hell out of here. And make sure he has the grimoire. We need that book." I still had no idea why, but I knew it was important.

We passed beneath the portico into the courtyard unscathed. I scanned every inch of the open space for possible attack. Nothing; there was nowhere for anyone to hide.

I was all set to yell "clear"—I'd obviously been watching too many cop shows—when a roar shook the courtyard, rattling my very bones. I glanced around wildly but other than me, Inigo, and Haakon, there was no one in sight.

"What the Hel was that?" Haakon shouted.

I didn't have time to answer. Another ear-splitting roar rattled the windows. A shape shifted out of nowhere. One minute nothing, the next a giant creature stood in front of us, its teeth dripping bloody saliva. It was a monster halfway between a Minotaur and a demon, eight feet tall at least and nearly as wide.

The top half was bull-like with horns so sharp it could spit a goat. Or a Hunter. The fur was shaggy and dark, trailing midway down the beast's chest, and the nostrils were wide and flared. The teeth, however, were pure demon, sharp and jagged.

The bottom half was sort of human-shaped but with cloven hooves for feet and yellowish skin that looked reptilian. The hands were human, too, except they ended in long, razor-sharp nails.

"Holy shit!" Inigo yelled. "What is that thing?"

I had no idea. I'd never seen anything like it. "Shift!" I yelled.

He didn't even ask. In a split second, there was a dragon the size of a horse sitting where Inigo had once stood, its blue scales shimmering aqua in the greenish light. Haakon's eyes widened, but otherwise he appeared unsurprised. Although he'd sensed Inigo's true nature, I doubted he'd ever seen a dragon shift before. It was a pretty amazing sight.

The beast snarled at Inigo's new form, snapping its jaws hungrily. Haakon slipped a shorter half sword out of the sheath at his side. I guessed he wasn't taking any chances. I pulled a gun from where it rested against the small of my back. It was loaded with lead, which wouldn't kill a Sidhe but would slow it down. Would it work on the creature?

I raised my arm and fired a single bullet straight into the monster's brain. The bullet ricocheted off the thing's skull and smacked into the wall. The beast whirled on me and roared again. Guess not. The bullet hadn't even penetrated bone. All I'd done was piss it off. I reached down and pulled a blade from my boot. The Sidhe-crafted metal glinted in the sunlight.

With another earth shattering roar, the beast charged.

Chapter 8

The Minotaur demon thing thundered across the slippery black paving stones, steam trailing from its wide, red nostrils. It let out a bellow as it picked up speed, heading toward me like a freight train. I shot again; this time the bullet went into its shoulder. Nothing. It didn't even pause despite the blood pouring out. Shit.

A split second before I became demon meat, I dove out of the way, hitting the paving stones and sliding on my belly through fetid slime. Wonderful. There went another pair of jeans.

The Minotaur demon let out an angry roar, its hooves scrambling against the cobblestone in an attempt to find footing. I rolled onto my side so I could see what was happing. Last thing I needed was to get gored in the back. Not a good way to end a trip through fairy land.

Slowed down by poor traction, the beast was still trying for me, straining with every ounce of strength in its body. Duh. I'd put a bullet in it. It was probably pissed as hell, although from what I could tell, the wound was already healing. Fortunately for me I had backup. Inigo, in dragon form, flew above its head, slashing with claw and teeth, shooting fire, which had little effect except to piss off the beast even more.

Haakon, on the other hand, was having more luck. Each slash of his sword opened a wide gash, spilling more dark blood onto the ground, where it mixed with the black slime. But it wasn't killing the thing. Each slash caused the creature pain, but it also healed in a matter of seconds. Then again, Haakon wasn't carrying a Sidhe blade.

I stared at the blade in my hand. Six inches of cold, fae steel. Would it even work on this beast? I mean, I could kill a Sidhe with it, but a monster like this? And what about the demon aspect? Was it really a demon? If so, that was a whole other kind of killing.

I strode toward the three figures and jumped into the fray. Inigo saw what I meant to do and lowered his tail enough so I could grab the tip of it. A quick flick, and I flew through the air. I landed a bit harder than I meant to, but I was where I wanted to be: on the humped back of the Minotaur demon. I grabbed onto its horns as it reared back, trying to throw me off. Guess it didn't like having a girl on top.

With a grin, I stabbed the blade deep into the soft spot between skull and ear. The thing shuddered, staggering to its knees, keening in pain. I yanked the blade out and thrust again. It shook its giant head, trying to dislodge me. I hung on to the hilt and the horns for dear life, squeezing my legs tight around its middle. When it stopped shaking, I yanked out the blade again, preparing for another thrust. With a massive shake, it sent me flying across the courtyard. I tumbled to a stop next to the fountain, shaking my head. Gods, that hurt.

Inigo and Haakon continued their onslaught, but the beast never wavered. It was clear I'd done some damage, but not enough. Not nearly enough. Regular weapons weren't hurting it. A Sidhe blade hadn't done anything. Heck, even a dragon couldn't bring the monster down. It was not of Sidhe, that was for certain.

I had no salt on me. That would banish a demon in a hurry. But I had something else. Carefully I pulled my amulet from where it always remained tucked beneath my shirt, close to my skin. I'd never used it to banish a demon before, but Eddie had told me the amulet, like my powers, was Atlantean in origin. Power was something a demon could understand. If it was a demon.

I stood, bracing my feet a couple feet apart. The stone in the center of the amulet was already glowing a soft blue, as it always did in the presence of Sidhe magic. I was still lightly channeling Earth, for all the good it was doing me. I reached down into myself and chose Fire. After all, that's where a demon returned to. I breathed in, breathed out, and pulled out the Fire. It ripped down my arms, a wild, living flame. Almost sentient. I burned with it, but it did not consume me. I felt nothing but warmth. This was my power, although it was the one over which I had dleast control.

Using the grounding influence of Earth and the wild hunger of Fire, I drew a ball of flame into my hand. The burning orb spun a few inches above my palm, the heat sizzling against my skin.

The stone in the Atlantean amulet now blazed like a blue sun, giving my flame a bluish tinge. Its power pulsed through me.

"Out of the way, boys," I shouted. They glanced at me. Haakon's eyes widened, and he quickly backed off. Inigo didn't move, just gave a dragon roar. Right. My Fire couldn't hurt him.

I flung the ball of Fire straight at the Minotaur demon. Clearly not as dumb as it looked, the beast whirled to the side. My fireball caught it in the backside instead of the head, but if the howl was anything to go by, I'd definitely caused it pain. A thick haze of smoke covered the creature's back, then it cleared. Holy hell, there was a gaping hole in its hide. I'd burned down to gleaming white bone. It stumbled sideways, falling on the uninjured side, though it still scrambled toward me, pulling itself along with its hands while dragging its rear. More smoke billowed from its nostrils.

I formed another fireball and lobbed it at the thing's head. It tried to duck, but it was too late. It let out a gods-awful shriek, and then the courtyard fell unnaturally silent. The beast was nothing more than a smoking ruin. I stared at it, trying to wrap my head around what I'd just done.

Inigo flapped down to the courtyard, landing with the screech of talons on stone. A shimmer of blue, and he was back in human form. Haakon kept his blades at the ready, eyes narrow, focused on the remains of the demon Minotaur, but the creature didn't move.

"What the Hel was that?"

I shrugged. "Demon of some kind, I think."

"In the Otherworld?" Inigo frowned. "I didn't think they could survive long here."

I hadn't realized he knew so much about the realm of the Sidhe. "No clue. All I know is it's here, and it's dead. Let's go find Alister." And my bet was that someone had brought it here just for us. Lucky us. The others nodded, and we crossed the courtyard and entered the palace.

Things had changed since my last visit. The halls had twisted and warped, resembling a fun house at a carnival. The marble, once black shot with gold, was simply flat black and oozing the same muck as the walls outside. Everything stank, the stench intensifying the deeper we traveled into the castle. Rot had set into fairy land. But why? Was it because Alister was here? Surely not. He was only human, after all. Doubtful he could affect the Otherworld in such a way.

"It's her," Inigo whispered. "The Queen." I noticed he didn't speak her name out loud. Wise man. "She's turned bad, and it's effecting all of faerie."

Haakon nodded. "It happened once, long ago. When her father was still on the throne. They say he went bad. Nearly took the Kingdom with him."

"Crap. And now it's happening again." Why wasn't I surprised? Oh, yeah: because Morgana had lost her ever lovin' mind and started a war with the djinn. "Well, we're not here to fix the Otherworld. We're here to find Alister and get back the grimoire."

"This would go faster if we spread out," Haakon suggested.

"Said the first guy to die in every horror movie ever made," Inigo mumbled.

I rolled my eyes. "This isn't a horror movie. And he's right. The palace is huge. We'll cover more ground this way."

"I'm not leaving you, Morgan," Inigo said firmly. "Not again."

It was no time for my heart to get all squidgy on me. "Fine. Inigo and I will take the south side of the castle. You take north," I told Haakon.

He gave me a snappy salute. "Yes, ma'am."

# # #

The wide corridors echoed with our footsteps, magnifying them until the sound made my ears ache. With every step deeper into the twisting heart of Morgana's castle, I felt eyes on us, watching our every move. I swore I caught movement out of the corner of my eye, but when I turned to look, there was nothing there. I would have sent out my Darkness, but I was afraid of what would happen in such an evil place. What if the Darkness liked it too much, and I lost control for good? A sick feeling roiled in the pit of my stomach. I hadn't felt this way at all the last time I'd been to the Otherworld.

"You sure are jumpy," Inigo said, his voice low. He never took his eyes off the hallway, scanning every nook and cranny for enemies.

"Aren't you? This place gives me the creeps."

His eyes darted to and fro, taking in everything around him. "There's nothing here. Nothing alive."

"Surely you can't sense the whole castle."

"No, but I can sense everything near us, and there is no one watching us. No one following us. We're alone."

Alone. Now there was a word to send shivers down your spine. If only we weren't rambling around a castle in the middle of the Otherworld. A castle whose owner had my name on her hit list. Not that she wanted to kill me, exactly. She would rather use me. And kill everyone I loved. Not my idea of a BFF.

"I swear someone's watching us."

"If there is someone, I can't sense them."

Freaking fantastic.

The long corridor had only a single door at one end. No other doors or windows. No staircases. Nothing. Just endless black walls oozing stinky goop. It seemed like hours before we reached that door, but it was probably only a couple minutes. At last we reached it and I pushed it open. It led into another corridor, but this one was lined with high windows on one side overlooking the violent river beneath. The other side was more blank wall.

"This isn't right," Inigo murmured.

"What do you mean?"

"The route we took should have led us back to the entrance of the castle. It's like the corridors have rerouted themselves."

"This isn't an episode of your favorite sci-fi show," I said. "Not a blue box in sight. Corridors just don't reroute themselves. There are laws of physics, you know."

He shook his head. "This is the Otherworld, remember? They've got their own laws, and they've nothing to do with our version of physics."

Damn Morgana. This was her doing. "Let's try going back the way we came."

But the door we'd come through was gone. "Up to her old tricks, I see," Inigo muttered. "Now what?"

"Why don't we fly?"

He eyed the windows. "I won't be able to fit through in dragon form. I'll have to jump out human and change mid-flight."

I felt a little sick at the thought. "Holy shit. You can do that?"

He gave me a nonchalant shrug. "It's a dragon thing."

I snorted. "Please don't kill yourself. I only just got you back." When in doubt, pretend everything's cool.

"I have no intention of dying," he said huskily. "I've got too many plans." He leaned forward and gave me a quick, hard kiss. "Bust out the window, love."

I nodded and pulled my gun from the waistband of my jeans. Using the butt, I smashed it hard against the window. The glass cracked but didn't break. Another couple of good smacks, and it shattered to bits. The tiny pieces of glass fell to the stone floor, glinting like diamonds in the weak sun.

"Here goes nothing." Inigo climbed up onto the windowsill and then stepped off like he was going for a stroll. Heart in my mouth, I rushed to the opening and looked down. There was no sign of him. Then I heard a triumphant howl.

Glancing up, I saw Inigo silhouetted against the greenish sky. He swooped and dove through the air, happy to be flying.

"Down here, you big lug," I shouted. I couldn't help the grin plastered across my face.

With another bellow, he dove toward the open window, pulling up a split second before he smacked his face into the side of the castle. Flying beneath the window, he hovered in place. I carefully lowered myself onto his back, grabbing onto the fold behind his neck with all my might.

Easy, love, you're going to strain something. His voice in my head was amused. How long had it been since we had been able to mind speak? My heart gave a painful lurch.

Shut up and fly, dragon boy.

Inigo dropped like a stone. My heart flew into my throat, and I let out an embarrassing squeal. Then he zoomed up high into the sky until the castle shrank to the size of a dollhouse behind us.

Show off.

I swear I heard him laughing in my head. He wheeled and began a leisurely flight toward the castle. I glanced below. All around lay wide green fields and thick forests, wide rivers and small lakes. Only instead of gleaming blue like water should, it was brown and brackish.

Wheeling again, Inigo swooped down over the castle. He circled it once.

Do you sense Alister?

Inigo waggled his big head back and forth in the negative. Damn. I hadn't seen any sign of Alister either. Inigo slowed as he spiraled toward the courtyard, landing with a slight jar. I tumbled off him onto the pavers as Haakon exited the building.

"Any sign?" he asked, not even blinking at the sight of me flying a dragon. Or more accurately, me falling off a dragon.

"Negative. We even circled the building from above. Inigo sensed nothing."

Inigo shimmered back to human form. "There's no sign he was ever here. The only humans I smell are the two of you."

I started to argue for three, but realized what I was saying. Inigo was only half-human, after all. "This was a trap. Morgana set up some dipshit fairy to lead us here, then placed that demon Minotaur thing to kill us." I ignored their flinches at the mention of the bitch queen's name.

"Didn't do much of a job." Haakon didn't relax, swords at the ready.

"Maybe she only expected me to come."

"Even so, she knew you could kill that thing," Inigo pointed out.

"Exactly. But she wants me alive so...not a trap so much as a distraction. But from what?"

"The war?" Haakon suggested.

"But she knows I won't involve myself, regardless of what she wants. Keeping me away from the battlefield accomplishes nothing."

"Unless she's got something else nasty up her sleeve," Inigo pointed out.

He'd made a good point. "Whatever. The beast is dead, and there's no sign of Alister or that damn grimoire. It's time to go home." And figure out what Morgana was up to.

"Can you open the portal from here?" Inigo asked.

I shrugged. "No idea. The last time I didn't need to create one from scratch. It was already open."

"So you have no idea if you can get us back," Haakon said. Well, it was more of a snap, but I didn't want to be uncharitable.

"Don't panic yet. Give me a moment."

I called the Earth power, pulling it out to shimmer along my body. I coiled it into my hands, imagining it forming a ball much like my fireballs. It spun in my hands, an orb of glowing green. I focused as hard as I could, picturing it turning into a portal. Nothing. The orb spun in lazy circles, waiting.

I reached deeper into my power, trying to connect it to that of the Otherworld. I visualized the power surging through me, connecting to the orb, creating a portal. Sweat popped out on my forehead, but otherwise, nothing happened.

Taking another breath, I tried again. And again. I called on my power until I was shaking with exhaustion and dark spots danced in front of my eyes.

"Look. Something's happening," Inigo shouted.

The orb had risen about two feet above my hands and turned more silver than green. It flattened out into a disc which stretched and twisted in midair before finally *poofing* out of existence. I stared at the empty space and felt like I was about to cry.

"Try again," Haakon urged.

"I can't." I said, swiping my hair out of my face. "I'm just not strong enough."

We were trapped.

Chapter 9

"What do you mean, 'we're trapped?'" The look on Haakon's face was definitely not one of giddy joy. "Trapped, as in we can't leave the castle trapped? Or trapped, as in we're stuck in the Otherworld for the next thousand years trapped?"

"Kind of the latter," I admitted.

"You said," he practically hissed in my face, "you could reopen the portal."

Boy, he was pissed. I couldn't say I blamed him. I had claimed I could open the portal. I'd more or less done it once before. Sort of.

"Listen, this isn't some magic wish thing. Wave my wand and voilà, portal!" I snapped back. "I'm doing the best I can."

"Well, your best isn't good enough," he snarled.

"Children," Inigo interrupted calmly. "Might we argue about this elsewhere? As Morgan pointed out earlier, this castle gives me the creeps."

Haakon glanced around the place like another demon might pop out and drag him to a Hel dimension or something. "Fine," he reluctantly agreed. "Let's get out of here. But we need a plan."

Inigo looked to me. "Morgan? You're the only one of us who's been here before."

I sighed. "I guess we go back to where Emory's portal opened. Maybe there's, I don't know, some residual energy left, and I can reopen that one."

"Why didn't we do that in the first place?' Haakon grumped.

"Because," I said, "it's faster to open a new one. Or it would be if I could have opened it," I admitted.

He snorted.

"Don't be an ass," I snapped. "The point is that theoretically you should be able to open a portal anywhere. Especially one to the Otherworld. They have a tendency to roam around. I should have been able to activate one right here with no problem." I shrugged. "But clearly that isn't happening."

"Clearly." Haakon's tone was dry as dust.

I started to retort, but Inigo slid his hand in mine and gave it a squeeze. Okay, so I didn't need to argue. Maybe Haakon was being a bit of a jerk, but I supposed I would be too if I found myself stuck in another dimension with no way home after someone had promised they could get me back. So, all in all, it was really sort of my fault. We tromped across the bridge. As we stepped onto the other side, there was no sign of our winged friend from earlier, which was probably a good thing. Haakon would probably smash it like a bug.

"Guess your little fairy friend didn't feel like hanging around," Inigo murmured.

"It accomplished what it came for. Why would it?" I had half a mind to call that little brat and give it a smackdown myself. But it wasn't the bug's fault. Morgana wasn't the kind of person you said no to if you wanted to live a long and healthy life. Then again, the tiny fae had taken a great deal of glee out of the whole thing, so maybe it did deserve a little smack.

We were almost to the tree line when the sound of a trumpet rang across the hillside. "What the hell was that?" I spun around looking for the source but saw nothing. I couldn't even pinpoint where it had come from.

"Hunting horn," Haakon said grimly.

"Somebody's after somebody," Inigo mused.

"Yeah. Us, no doubt. We better move our asses." I took off for the trees, the boys jogging along behind me.

I dodged under the nearest branch and glanced behind us. Still nothing, although I heard thunder in the distance. Must be a storm coming. I glanced at the sky, then frowned. Nope. Not a storm. Another look behind us, and I realized where the sound was coming from: the Queen's Guard in full armor mounted on freaking unicorns and charging us. I was pretty sure it wasn't a welcoming party.

"Move it," I shouted. "Lose them in the trees."

We raced into the forest, branches swatting us, vines curling around arms and legs trying their best to slow us down. I slid my fairy blade out and hacked at a particularly vicious vine. This was going to take forever, but at least it meant the unicorns wouldn't be able to follow us. Their riders would have to hang back or dismount, which was a good thing. I so did not want to deal with unicorn horns. Those things were sharp.

"Behind me," I ordered. Points to them; they didn't even question me, just fell into line.

With the blade connecting me to the magic of the Otherworld, I beckoned my Earth power, yanking it out of my center with absolutely zero ceremony. It roared through me like the Fire would. It was just one minute things were normal and the next I was glowing. Green no less. At least I matched the rest of the bloody world.

Immediately the vines and branches snapped back, parting the way for us to shove through. Mentally I ordered them to close behind us. Amazingly, they did, barring the way of the guard.

I heard curses in Sidhe as the Queen's Guard was forced to dismount in order to pursue us into the forest. In front of us was a wide path, behind a twisted bramble. I heard the sound of our pursuers hacking away at the undergrowth. Good luck to 'em.

I was starting to sweat. Quickly tiring of the dual effort of maintaining control over fairy flora while running for my life, I tripped over a root — no doubt it had done it deliberately—and nearly fell flat on my face. Inigo grabbed me and hauled me up, keeping hold on me to tow me along behind him.

"I can shift," he said, barely winded. "Fight them off a bit longer."

"No. I'm fine. The forest will keep them back." At least I hoped it would. "We have to get to the right spot."

Haakon said nothing, just barged ahead of us with grim determination. The man clearly wanted the hell out of Dodge. Can't say I blamed him.

We finally burst from the forest to where I was pretty sure Emory had opened the original portal. Sure enough, the magic I was channeling picked up residual energy from it. The glow of my amulet intensified.

"This is it," I panted.

"Can you open it?" Haakon demanded.

"I don't know yet. Geez, in a hurry much?"

"Yes," he snapped. "I really do think we should hurry."

I followed the direction of his gaze and sure enough, I saw the glint of armor through the trees. Damn, they'd gotten through faster than I thought.

Exhausted but determined, I concentrated on the residual energy of the portal. Focusing as hard as I could, I drew the dissipated energy back together, binding it with both my Earth magic and the magic of the Otherworld. Slowly, painfully slowly, it formed a ball of energy and then spun itself into a shimmering disc. The portal was open.

"Go," I shouted at Inigo and Haakon.

"You first," Inigo insisted.

"I go through and the portal closes. Get your asses moving."

Haakon didn't need a second urging. He jumped headlong into the portal, disappearing. Inigo paused long enough to press a hard kiss on my lips before jumping in himself.

The Queen's Guard crashed through the forest, the beat of booted feet on solid ground as they hurried toward me. I spun around. At the front of the charge was the captain of the

Queen's Guard, Kalen. His shoulder-length blond hair shone greenish-gold in the sunlight, though I knew it to be true gold, and his eyes flashed an angry violet. His knuckles turned white around the hilt of his sword. He and I had had a run-in once before. I'd gotten away that time, too. I paused long enough to give him a wide smile and a little finger wave before I stepped backward into the portal.

# # #

I tumbled, almost falling over someone. In front of me, the portal blinked out, and I breathed a sigh of relief. I glanced around to see who I'd tripped over. Haakon was sprawled on the floor, shaking his head.

I snorted. "That's what you get for jumping in headfirst."

Inigo struggled to hold back a laugh. "You all right?"

"Fine. They'd just broken through when I stepped in. You should have seen the look on Kalen's face."

"Kalen?" He lifted an eyebrow but otherwise seemed unperturbed.

"Captain of the Queen's Guard. He and I have a bit of a rivalry going. He took me prisoner. I stole Darroch from under his nose." I shrugged. "You know how it is."

He rolled his eyes. "Yeah." He leaned forward and pressed his forehead to mine, cupping my cheeks in his hands. "Glad you're okay."

"Would you two get a room?" Haakon staggered to his feet. "We need to figure out what to do next."

Oh, yeah. Alister. I looked around. We were back in Emory's Wiccan chamber, or whatever she called it. She was nowhere to be seen. Probably out front with customers or whatnot. "Let's find Emory. Maybe she can help."

The three of us tromped through the storeroom into the

main shop. Several pairs of wide eyes stared at us. What? Hadn't they ever seen a woman with a couple of hotties bristling with swords? Okay, probably not. One of the women, probably in her early seventies and sporting a hot pink perm, clutched at her pearls as she stared at Haakon. I seriously thought she was going to pass out. Or jump him. It could have gone either way.

"Ladies," Haakon nodded gallantly to each in turn. I swear I heard someone let out a tiny squee. Guess they'd have quite a tale for their next Bunco night.

Emory finished ringing up a sale and then marched over to us, her skirts swishing angrily. "Do you mind?" she hissed. "You're disturbing my customers."

"Yeah, sorry about that," I whispered, "but I don't think it's in a bad way."

Inigo was flirting outrageously with a woman about my mother's age, gushing over some kind of soap or other. The woman already had at least half a dozen bars in her basket and was adding more. Haakon stood stoically while most of the rest of the women gawked at him or busied themselves pretending not to gawk. Wow, those shopping baskets were filling with goodies.

She glanced around. "Fine. Whatever. But you've got to get them out of here before people ask too many questions."

"I will, but first I need your help. We couldn't find Alister. He wasn't there. It was all a trick."

"Figures. Queen Bitch is brilliant at that."

"Yeah, so I need to find out where he might go next. Could you scry for him?"

"That didn't turn out so well the last time."

She had a point. "I don't know what else to try."

"Okay, okay. But later. Meet me at the house at nine-thirty tonight. Now get them out of here before I have a riot on my hands."

Chapter 10

Emory's house looked even creepier at night than it did in broad daylight. Talk about a clichéd place for a witch to live. It was straight out of some '50s *B* movie.

It was an old Victorian complete with curlicues along the porch railing and an actual turret. Unfortunately, it had seen better days. Even in the dark I could see the paint was peeling clean off the wood siding, and there were gaps where the porch boards had rotted. A couple of the windows had been boarded up, no doubt thanks to vandals mistaking the place as abandoned. The small front garden had probably once been quite beautiful, but the roses had turned to brambles and nearly overgrown the rusted wrought iron fence.

Inside was little better. There were wide swaths of random colors painted on the walls of the foyer, and the stairs were missing the bannister. A bare bulb dangled from the ceiling, casting eerie shadows.

"Sorry about the mess," Emory said, waving her hand airily around the entry. "I'm remodeling. Do you know how hard it is to pick out a paint color?"

"Pretty hard I guess." If the rainbow of reds, blues, and taupe was anything to go by. The guys didn't say anything. Smart guys.

"Some idiot replaced the chandelier in the '70s. Ghastly thing. I had to take it down. Haven't found the perfect replacement yet, but not to worry. I will."

I'm not sure why she thought I would be worried about her chandelier, but whatever. "So, this scrying thing," I urged as I followed her into what I could only assume had once been a living room. Newspapers covered every inch of floor space, and random bulky shapes loomed beneath drop cloths. More wild paint test colors smeared the walls. Haakon leaned against the doorframe while Inigo prowled the room. Looking for what, I had no idea.

"Yeah, the scrying thing. Look...." She turned and faced me. "I'm not terribly comfortable with this. That Alister Jones person gives me the heebie jeebies."

"You think he gives you the heebie jeebies? Imagine what he does to me. I've got to find that bastard before he does something bad. I mean, worse."

She nodded grimly. "This may not work, you know. I've got lots of skills, but scrying isn't my best one. Plus you know how it went the last time."

"Just try, okay?"

"I've been doing a little research. I think I might be able to boost the energy and get a better pinpoint. Weave through some of the muck he's putting into the universe. But I'm going to need help."

"Whatever you need."

She smiled. "I need the three of you to help me form a circle."

"No problem," I said. Inigo quickly joined us, but Haakon hesitated. He didn't look pleased. "Get your Viking butt over here," I ordered. "We've got stuff to do. No time to coddle your delicate sensibilities."

He snorted in derision but joined us in the center of the room. Emory disappeared through the wide doorway and return with a crystal and her computer pad.

"Aren't you worried about the neighbors?" Inigo asked, glancing toward the large window. It opened to the street, no curtains or blinds to block the view of curious onlookers.

She laughed. "Wards. All they'll see is a bunch of people sitting around chatting and drinking tea."

She must have some serious juju to create wards that strong. Kabita couldn't do it, and she was one of the most powerful witches I knew. Okay, so other than Emory, she was the only witch I knew, but that was beside the point.

Emory had us sit around in a circle with our knees nearly touching. I had no problem with it, and neither did Inigo, but Haakon looked distinctly uncomfortable. I wasn't sure if it was because he wasn't into witchy things or that his six foot, five inch frame didn't fold up as easily as the rest of us did. Maybe he had the hots for Emory, although the vibes I was getting weren't quite the these-people-are-going-to-rip-each-other's-clothes-off type. Possibly it was because Emory made him leave his sword by the door. He probably felt naked.

I blinked. Yeah. I should stop right there.

After casting the circle, Emory placed the pad in the center with the map program up. "All right, everyone hold hands. Inigo and Haakon, place yours on my knees. I need mine free."

Inigo looked a little awkward putting his hand on a virtual stranger's knee, but all for the greater good, right? Haakon looked even more uncomfortable. Seriously, were all Sunwalkers this uptight?

"Do not break the circle until I tell you. And don't talk to me while I'm casting."

We nodded obediently.

"Let us begin."

She began to hum and then to mumble. Sort of an English/Atlantean hybrid, if I wasn't mistaken. Her eyes took on a faraway look, and one hand drifted into the air as if she saw something there and was trying to grasp it. Her second hand rose as if of its own volition. It looked like she was moving things around in midair except there was nothing there.

"What is she doing?" I hissed.

"Weaving a spell," Haakon whispered back.

"What?"

"She's a spellwalker."

Inigo and I stared at him. Inigo looked as confused as I felt. "Spellwalker?" we said at the same time.

Emory made an annoyed sound, and we lowered our voices. "Surely you've heard of them?"

Inigo and I shook our heads.

Haakon sighed. "It's a kind of witch."

I frowned. "There are different kinds of witches?"

He nodded. "As there are different kinds of Hunters."

Touché.

"So, what does that have to do with whatever she's doing?" I asked, nodding at Emory, whose movements had increased in speed as if she was creating some kind of pattern and had to do it fast. Her eyes had that glazed look people get when they're daydreaming.

"Spellwalkers are very rare. She's the first I've seen in...a very long time. They can essentially see the components of spells as if they are physical entities. They can walk among the elements of a spell, manipulating them as they do their spell work. It allows them to create unbelievably powerful spells. Much more than any ordinary witch."

Seriously cool.

"If you are all done jabbering, I'd like to cast my spell now." Emory's voice held a dreamy quality, but it was still a little on the sharp side.

We shut up. With a smile she pulled some invisible thing out of the air and threw it at the pad. The map jumped and the crystal lying next to it began to glow. Emory picked up the crystal, and still mumbling strange words, allowed the crystal to hover over the map.

The crystal began swinging in a wide arc, but no matter what, it wouldn't settle. My back ached, my knees were cramping, and still nothing happened.

Finally Emory sat back with a sigh. "Sorry, Morgan. It isn't going to work. Whatever he's doing to mask himself is working far too well. Without knowing which spell he's using, I can't break it."

Bugger. Back to square one. "Thanks for trying anyway. It was worth a shot."

She gave me a lopsided smile and banished the circle. I staggered to my feet, feeling blood rushing back a little too fast. Inigo braced me, his hands warm on my back. I reveled in having him here where he belonged. So he wasn't one hundred percent the happy-go-lucky Inigo I'd first fallen in love with, but I didn't expect that. He might be different, darker, but he was still mine. Tears pricked at my eyelids.

"I think we should all rest tonight and start fresh in the morning," Haakon suggested. It surprised me. I'd expected him to be all gung-ho.

"I agree," Inigo said, his voice a low rumble behind me. "We're all exhausted."

"I will walk," Haakon said. "My hotel is not far from here." He had a hotel already? When had that happened? "I could use a bit of fresh air."

"I'll take Morgan home."

I raised an eyebrow. I was thoroughly ignored.

"Shall we meet for breakfast?" Haakon asked.

"At my house," I suggested. "I'll make pancakes."

He nodded. "See you at seven."

I snorted. "Make that nine and you're on." Seven, my ass.

He smiled a little. "Very well, see you then."

We left Emory's, and Haakon took off down the street, fading into the night. I was unaware of any hotels nearby. Where the hell was he staying? Inigo opened the passenger door of my Mustang and waved me in. I didn't argue. I was so tired my limbs were shaking. How was he not tired?

Oh, yeah. He hadn't been the one channeling superpowers

all day. In fact, shifting in and out of dragon form seemed to energize him.

Inigo pulled into my drive and shut off the engine. "Can I come in? We need to talk."

I stared at him for a moment. The last time he'd said those words, I'd felt nothing but dread. This time, oddly, I felt hope.

"Of course."

Inside, I brewed a pot of decaf coffee. Normally I wouldn't touch the stuff, but at this point, regular would keep me up all night, and I desperately needed sleep.

"What do we need to talk about?" I asked, watching the pot brew, studiously ignoring his nearness.

He placed his hands on my shoulders and gently turned me around. "Morgan, I am sorry."

I swallowed. "For what?" I needed him to spell it out.

"For leaving you. For shutting you out. For hurting you. I was so...lost. Confused. Angry and...I don't even know. I couldn't deal with anything. I didn't know how. If I had it all to do over again..." He shrugged. "I'd probably do the same damn thing. But the truth is, without you, Morgan, I'm lost. I'm not myself. I'm not..." He seemed to search for the world. "Complete."

I swallowed. "I get it. You were hurting. I just wish you would have let me help you."

He smiled sadly. "Me, too. But I couldn't. I don't know why. I can't explain it. All I know is I am here now. This is where I want to be. With you always if you'll have me."

"Are you proposing?" Me and my big mouth.

He laughed softly. "If I was proposing, you'd know it. Consider this a pre-proposal. Until I'm back in your good graces. I'm pretty sure if I proposed now, I wouldn't like the answer."

He was right about that. "Okay."

"Okay?"

I nodded. "I accept your pre-proposal. But you'd better not shut me out again."

"Can't promise that. Not totally. But I will do my best, and I give you permission to call my ass on it if I'm doing it again."

"You better believe I will." I pulled him down to kiss him, and the minute our lips locked, my exhaustion fled. "Stay the night," I whispered.

"If you insist."

"I do."

Chapter 11

With infinite slowness I wound silk ribbons around Inigo's wrists before tying the ends to the bedposts. First the left hand, then the right. He watched me with heavy-lidded eyes. Promises of payback. We both knew he could get out of the ties if he wanted. We both knew he wouldn't.

I sat back to admire my handiwork. The gods' handiwork. Whatever. He was so fucking beautiful, he took my breath away. Made my chest a little tight. And this fucking beautiful man was in *my* bed, where he belonged.

I had no idea where I'd come up with the idea to tie him up, although I wasn't totally surprised he'd let me. Inigo had always been the playful type. Before.... I pushed the thoughts away. Damn, if I wasn't going to take advantage of the situation.

Where to start?

My breath traced the delicate shell of his left ear. He tensed between my thighs. My tongue followed. He sucked in a breath. I nuzzled that sweet spot behind the ear where the skin was so very tender. This time it was a moan.

I slid one hand into the thick tangle of his hair. In this light the golden strands looked darker. Almost brown. I pulled his head back a little, baring his throat. A smile hovered on my lips as I traced the sensitive space from ear to collarbone. Laving with tongue, nipping with teeth. He twisted a little against his bonds but didn't slip them. The thick length of him pressed hard against my inner thigh. I was swollen and wet. I wanted to push myself onto him, take him inside me and ride him until we both screamed. But I also wanted to play with him.

Play won.

His sapphire eyes burned with heat and need. I knew he was thinking about fucking me. But he also wanted me to play with him first. The old Inigo peeked from beneath sooty lashes as his eyes turned gold.

Play definitely won.

I nipped the tender skin along his collarbone. Soothed it with my tongue, drank in the musky scent of aroused man. Gods, he was delicious.

Letting go of his hair, I slid my left thumb over his right nipple. Toyed a little with the flat bud. He hissed, so I moved my mouth to his left nipple. The hiss grew into another moan. And then, "Yes." Clearly, he was into it. Good thing, because I was thoroughly enjoying myself as I paid equal attention to each nipple.

By now I was practically dripping with arousal. His writhing had brought his shaft solidly against my cleft. I wanted desperately to rub myself up and down his length, but if I did, I'd be a goner. Playtime would be over.

I wasn't ready for that. He deserved a little torture, and I deserved my fun.

I moved away, and he groaned in protest. "Morgan." My name was a breath on his lips.

"Patience," I whispered.

"Hurry," he said.

"Good things come to those who wait."

"They had better."

His trace of an accent drove me wild. That perfectly proper British was music to my ears. He knew what it did to me. Bastard.

"Be quiet," I said.

The smile he gave me was wicked. His golden eyes sparkled, and I knew he was thinking of escaping his bonds, but he didn't.

I kissed my way down over his flat belly. The short silky hairs trailing from his navel tickled my nose. The musky scent of him grew stronger.

I trailed my left hand down his body before wrapping it

around the base of his rigid shaft. "Gods, yes," he gasped, thrusting a little. I drew my tongue up his length from base to tip before swirling it over the smooth head, eliciting another eager moan. A few salty beads of moisture hit my taste buds. He tasted as good as he smelled. But this wasn't my goal. Not yet.

With my right hand, I cupped his heavy sac. Then I drew his balls into my mouth and sucked gently.

"Oh, gods."

I let his testicles fall. "You want me to stop."

"No," he panted. "Don't stop." His eyes were live coals. His cheeks were flushed. If I'd thought him beautiful before, it was nothing compared to what he was now. Perhaps absence did make the heart grow fonder, after all.

I went back to lavishing his balls with attention, drawing first one and then the other into my mouth. I sucked them gently, feeling them swell. He writhed beneath me, his knuckles hitting the headboard in frustration. Still he did not free himself. I knew he was on the brink.

I let his balls go, licking up his shaft again. Then I straightened up, letting go of him. His eyes caught mine, confused until I moved up his body, positioning myself over his tip.

Our eyes locked as I sank down onto him. Slowly, slowly, inch by inch. He was so thick, the fit was almost painfully tight, but I was so wet he slid in easily. By the time he was fully inside me, we were both panting with effort. We both wanted this to last. Neither of us was sure we could.

I slid myself back up to his tip, relishing the delicious friction. This time, I must have gone too far.

He was suddenly free of his bonds. His fingers dug into my hips as he grabbed me and slammed me back down onto him.

I wasn't sure whose cry of pleasure was louder, mine or his.

The pace he set was almost frantic, but it felt exactly right. It had been so long. Far too long. His every thrust into me sent waves of such intense pleasure pounding through me, I lost all ability to think. All I could do was hang on and feel every moment of ecstasy.

"Oh, gods, yes," I cried. "Harder." I bent forward so each downward thrust of my body would slam my bud against him. It was building, that pressure inside me. A few more thrusts, and I'd be over the edge.

I knew he was close, too. His grip on my hips was almost painful as he worked me up and down his length. Sweat beaded his forehead and upper lip as he ground into me. The cords in his throat stood out as he strained against his release. He was trying to make it last.

"Come for me."

His words undid me. I came so hard I thought I might split apart. It was like the insides of me burst open in one moment of such insane pleasure, it was almost pain. I cried out as orgasm swept over me. My inner muscles milked him as wave after wave swept through me. I'd never come like that before in my life.

I watched him come beneath me. That expression of agony and ecstasy on his face must have mirrored my own. He strained against me as he came inside me. A couple more thrusts, and he was done, though he gasped a little as the last few tremors of my body gripped him.

Still joined, I sank down on top of him, head pillowed on his chest. We lay there for a moment, both too exhausted to move.

Then one hand tangled in my hair, caressing my scalp. The other wrapped around me, holding me to him as if he would never let me go. Lips pressed against my forehead.

"You are amazing," he murmured, his accent thick, voice husky.

"Stay with me," I whispered, half-afraid he'd say no. That he'd go back to his apartment, leave me alone again.

His arms tightened around me as he whispered, "Always."

#

Sun slanted across my face, and I threw up my hand to block it. It was too damn early, but the scent of brewing coffee called me like a lover. I opened one eye. The clock said it was five to nine. Shit. Haakon would be here any second if he wasn't already. I needed to get my shit together.

I staggered out of bed and into the attached bathroom, did my business, and then jumped in the shower. I had just stepped out and wrapped a towel around me, my hair still dripping all over the floor, when I felt an odd, sucking pull. It felt as if someone, or something, was trying to pull me physically from the bathroom. What the hell?

I braced myself against the bathroom door feeling suddenly disoriented. What was going on?

"Inigo!" I shouted.

And then everything around me faded to black.

Chapter 12

I came to lying on a cold, hard floor. Had I passed out in the bathroom?

I placed my palm flat on the floor. Not tile. Stone. I pulled my hand away with a frown. Stinky black goo coated my skin. I stared at the wall about two inches from my face. Black and dripping with dark slime. I rolled over to find Morgana sitting a few feet away on an elegant, straight-backed chair. Behind her ranged the Queen's Guard, Kalen in the middle looking smug.

Shit. I was in the Otherworld.

"How the hell did I get here?" I snarled, sitting up. I realized I was still wearing nothing but a towel. Great. I was facing my arch nemesis half-naked. This was like a bad dream.

"How do you think you got here?" Morgana's tone was arch. "I brought you here, Hunter."

"Send me back. Now. Or I swear I will—"

"You will what? Kill me?" She laughed maniacally. Her usually shining hair was dull and brassy. Her eyes had gone from clear blue to some muddy, indeterminate color. She was still beautiful, but she was no longer breathtaking. "You don't have the guts."

I narrowed my eyes. "Oh, I've got the guts. Remember your brother, Albrecht?"

Her pale face grew whiter. "You did not kill my brother. The djinn king did."

It was true. The Marid had been the one to deal the fatal blow. "And yet, you've been blaming me. That's what this is about, isn't it? You've finally called in your marker." I knew it in my gut. Morgana, the crazy bitch, had been insisting I owed her for her brother's death. Never mind that had been her plan all along. And I'd owed her before that. For a "gift" she'd given me. One I hadn't wanted anyway. I'd been wondering when she'd get around to it.

"Spill it, Majesty. What do you want me to do?"

"I want you to end this war with the djinn."

I stared at her in confusion. "What do you think I've been trying to do? You're the one who started this damn war in the first place."

"No, Morgan. You aren't listening." She rose elegantly from her chair and strode toward me, her steps so light it looked as if she were gliding on air. "I want you to destroy the djinn."

"Oh, hell no. I am not your little puppet. I do not owe you anything."

A pool of ink-black water appeared suddenly between us. Oh, gods, not that damn pool. Morgana waved her hand above the water, and an image shivered into place. I saw Haakon and Inigo running around my house, searching for me. There was calm determination on Haakon's face and near panic on Inigo's. The focus zoomed in on his face. I swallowed bile.

"You finish this war, Hunter," Morgana hissed. "Or this time I finish the job."

My heart stopped beating for a split second and then burst into high gear. She'd ripped his heart out once. I would not let her do it again. My face flushed with rage as I rose to my feet, the towel dropping from my body. I ignored the fact I was naked in front of the perfect Queen of the Sidhe and her entire guard. Kalen and his men stared, some in awe, some in repulsion. For once I didn't care.

"Listen to me," I bit out, every word a laceration. "You will not touch him, or I will rip your kingdom apart." I'd never heard myself sound so cold. So deadly. The Darkness inside me rose, and Morgana must have seen in it my eyes. She trembled. The fairy queen, afraid of little old me. The Darkness wanted to laugh in triumph, but I controlled it. Barely.

"You dare threaten me?" Morgana spat.

"It's not a threat, Majesty." I made the title sound like a swear word. "It's a promise."

I reached down into myself and pulled out the Earth. It shimmered across my skin and spilled across the disgusting stone floor in delicate tendrils. It burrowed between the tiles of marble and curled up along the legs of the Queen's Guard. The Sidhe looked startled, terrified even, as the green mist that was my power surrounded them in coils.

For a moment, nothing else happened. And then I let loose. For the first time, I allowed the power of Earth free reign. It pulsed through me in roaring waves. Beneath my feet the ground began to quake. The castle shook to its very core, the decayed stone crumbling around us. The Queen's Guard, eyes glassy, drew their swords and advanced on the queen.

For once in her life, Morgana looked terrified. Actually scared. Could the Queen's Guard really kill her? The royals, according to what I'd heard, were the closest thing to truly immortal there was. The only thing in the known universe that could kill them was to use special handcuffs created of Sidhe steel and ancient magic to bind their powers, making them temporarily mortal. Then have an angry djinn in its demon form rip out their heart. I was fresh out of handcuffs and there weren't any djinn in the Otherworld. But could the Queen's Guard, armed with Sidhe blades, cause her enough harm to end her life or at least damage her? I was betting so, or she wouldn't have looked so frightened.

"Remember this, Morgana, the next time you decide to fuck with my people."

"Stop this now," a voice bellowed. I whirled to find Kalen glaring at me. He appeared to be frozen on the spot, but other than that, he was unaffected by my magic. I was stopping him, but I wasn't controlling him. Interesting.

The queen flushed angry red. "You," she spat. Not at me,

but at her captain. "Traitor."

"How can I be a traitor, my queen? Have I not served you well these many centuries?" His voice was calm, but there was something hard in his eyes. Curiouser and curiouser.

"This cannot be!" she shrieked. "I am the last. The only one."

I stared first at her, then at Kalen, then back again. The last what?

"Yes," Kalen said calmly. "You've killed all the others."

"And I will kill you, too." She was practically spitting now.

"Hey, if this is going to turn into some kind of bloodbath. I'd like to go home first and wash off this gunk. It stinks like a dead squirrel."

Morgana whirled on me as if suddenly remembering she had an audience. She gave an angry shriek and waved her hand. The next moment I was sprawled buck naked, covered in goo, across my bathroom floor.

"Well, shit. Now I'm going to have to mop."

"Morgan!" Inigo shouted as he came running from the bedroom. "Where have you been?"

"Long story," I said, staggering to my feet. "Right now I need another long hot shower and to get that crap cleaned off my floor."

"I'll get the mop, but please. What happened?"

I stepped into the shower, yanking the curtain closed behind me, and turned the spray on full blast. "Morgana is up to her usual stupid fairy tricks. She called in her so-called marker. She wants me to help her kill the djinn, or she's going to kill you for real this time."

A moment of silence from the other side of the shower curtain. "Um. So, what are you going to do?"

"Well, not planning on letting her kill you, if that's what you're worried about." I stuck my head out of the shower and grinned at him. "I showed her one of my magic tricks, and it sort of distracted her. For now anyway." I popped back under the hot spray. "But I discovered something really interesting."

"What's that?"

"Kalen, the captain of the Queen's Guard. I think he might be one of Morgana's relatives."

Chapter 13

Finally clean, I stepped out of the shower and wrapped myself in my pink, fluffy, totally non-sexy robe. One of those robes that made you look about two sizes bigger than you really are. It was warm and cozy, though. Exactly what I needed.

Inigo had finished cleaning, and the bathroom floor sparkled like new. The air smelled of sweet orange oil. Not a bit of dead-squirrel scent lingered. I wrapped my hair in a towel and padded to the kitchen, where I found Kalen perched on a chair staring at a mug of coffee like it might bite him. I wasn't sure if it was because he was using my Wonder Woman mug, or if he'd never had coffee before.

"What the ever loving crap is he doing here?"

Haakon shifted uncomfortably like he was afraid I might go off the deep end, but Inigo smiled and swooped in with a cup of coffee and a kiss. "He popped in while you were in the shower. He says he has some intel he wants to share with us. Now drink your coffee."

I took an obedient sip. It was perfect, with just the right proportions of half and half and raw sugar. That was one of the things I loved about Inigo. He paid attention. "If it's the thing about you being related to the queen, don't bother. I already know. Just not how, specifically."

Kalen shoved his coffee mug away and grinned. "Her nephew."

"Albrecht was your father?" Oh, great. Not another loony tune.

He shook his head, shoving his fingers through his tangled hair. It was like Morgana's, only a little more blond. How had I not noticed that before? His face didn't morph like normal Sidhe, either. I'd assumed it was because he was the captain of the Queen's Guard. I guessed the truth ran deeper than that.

"My mother was the queen's younger sister. She took a lover from among the Queen's Guard and for that my aunt had her executed." He stared grimly into his coffee for a moment. "She didn't know my mother had already given birth to me and hidden me with one of the mid-level Sidhe families that lurk around the throne. If the queen had known who I was, I'd have never made it to my first birthday."

"Oh, fantastic. So she really is crazy as a wombat."

"If you mean the current war with the djinn, then yes. It's lucky you can control the royal guard."

Haakon lifted an eyebrow. "You can control the Queen's Guard now?"

"Apparently." I took a sip of my coffee. Yep. Definitely perfect. I gave Inigo a grin, which he returned. My world might be crazy, but this, at least, was a bright shining spot in the midst of it.

"If you can control the guard, why not march them into battle and stop the other Sidhe from attacking the djinn? Put an end to this war once and for all?" Haakon asked.

"We've been through this already. I can control the Sidhe, but I can't control the djinn. I wouldn't be able to stop them annihilating the fae."

"I don't see the problem." He leaned against the counter, his face impassive. Gods, I hoped he wasn't really as cold as he sounded. Then again, Vikings were known for pragmatism and brutality. I didn't suppose a person gave that up because they lived a thousand years longer than they should.

"Not all Sidhe are bad because their queen is crazy. They don't deserve to die. The war has to be stopped another way."

"How do you know she's crazy? Maybe she's just evil." He eyed me over the rim of his mug. Was this some kind of test?

"She's a little of both," Kalen said as he got up to dump his now-cold beverage into the sink. What a waste of perfectly good coffee.

"What do you mean?" Inigo asked, taking a seat next to me at the table. He looked calm, peaceful. Happier than I'd seen him in a long time. It warmed me to my cockles. Whatever those were.

"The royal palace was once very different from what you saw," Kalen explained, pacing the small kitchen. "It was once alabaster shot with pink and gold. It was breathtaking, and its radiance could be seen for miles. The sunlight of the Otherworld was pure and bright."

"I don't see the point," Haakon groused.

"Jeez, let him tell us, won't you, Mr. Grumpy Pants?" I snapped. Inigo held back a smirk while Haakon looked affronted.

"The palace reflects the heart of its leader," Kalen continued. "That is the way of the Otherworld. When my grandparents ruled, it was bright and light. Until gray began to seep around the edges, revealing their decay. After my aunt killed the king and queen and took the throne, everyone thought it would go back to the way it was. But it didn't."

"It got worse," I murmured.

He nodded, taking a seat again. "Exactly." He leaned toward me, his expression intense. For the first time, I realized his eyes were the color of amethysts. I was quite certain the first time I'd seen him, his eyes had been green, like the forests of the Otherworld. "Which brings me to the reason I'm here."

"And what is that?" I asked, eyeing him carefully.

"I want you to help me take the throne."

# # #

"This is nuts," I mumbled. "I can't believe Kalen wants me to help him usurp the throne of Sidhe. He's as crazy as his aunt."

Inigo gave me a sidelong glance. "Possibly not."

I took my eyes off the road long enough to shoot him a glare. He was looking particularly tasty in a pair of snug jeans, a soft blue T-shirt that set off his eyes, and a brown leather jacket. I noticed he was less flamboyant these days. I had no idea if it was because of what we'd been through, or because we were together. "What do you mean?"

"Think about it. Mor—the queen—has wrecked Fairy. We saw it. The place is turning into a hellhole, and there's nothing anyone can do about it. Except Kalen. He's the natural heir to the throne. Maybe he can reverse the damage. Seems like he wants to, and I'm pretty sure he's still sane."

"Pretty sure isn't exactly a glowing recommendation."

He shrugged. "We know the queen is a lunatic. Getting her out of the way sounds like a good plan."

"What if Kalen is worse? Sometimes it's better to go with the devil you know." Although I wasn't sure I believed that. Not in this case.

"Sometimes you gotta take some risks."

He had a point. I sighed and pressed down on the accelerator. We were on our way to meet Trevor at the airport. I'd told Kalen I'd think about his request if he helped find Alister. Kalen had admitted Alister had been to the Otherworld, but he'd left. Kalen didn't know where he'd gone. He did know that Brent Darroch—the man who'd tried to kill me and steal the Atlantean amulet—had been in on the escape plan and was supposed to have broken out of prison along with Alister, but good ol' Alister had left him behind. Figured. We were hoping Darroch would be pissed off enough to spill the proverbial beans on the delightful Mr. Jones. It had worked with Jade, Alister's protégée. For her help, she'd been downgraded from high security to a more comfortable location away from Area 51.

Trevor was the only person who could get us into Area 51 to question Darroch. I'd asked him about doing a Skype call—I was getting tired of trips to the Nevada desert—but Trevor had said prisoners had no access to the internet. For good reason. So it was off to the middle of nowhere once again.

Trevor was standing next to a black SUV when we pulled into the private airstrip. His mirrored shades were firmly in place, and his dark suit was perfectly pressed. His pristine white shirt set off his latte skin to perfection. He looked like he'd just stepped out of GQ Magazine.

"You don't look like you've been fending off Sidhe warriors," I said as he opened my car door and gave me a bear hug.

"Looks can be deceiving, sister mine." He pulled off his shades, and there were dark circles under his brown eyes.

"You look like hell."

"Gee, thanks."

"Sure. Anytime. That it?" I asked, nodding toward the tiny, baby plane-let. The previous times we'd been to Area 51, we'd flown commercial and then driven across the desert, but time was of the essence.

"That's it. We've got permission to use the airstrip on the base. We'll be in and out in no time."

"Good. I've still got a damn war to deal with."

As we strode toward the plane, Trevor gave me a look. "You think you're the only person who can stop this war?"

I frowned at his snarky tone. "I don't. But Morgana seems to think so."

Trevor and Inigo looked around wildly, as if the queen herself would suddenly appear at the sound of her name. It was a reasonable fear. She did have a habit of doing that.

"What do you mean?" Trevor asked.

As we buckled ourselves into the insanely posh leather seats,

I told him about Morgana pulling me into the Otherworld. About calling in the "favor" I supposedly owed her, and how she had ordered me to help her destroy the djinn.

"Is that even possible?" he asked.

I shrugged, snuggling into my seat. "I wouldn't have thought so. The Marid, at least, can actually control my powers. So I can't see what I can do. I am able to control the Queen's Guard and some of the other Sidhe, but that won't do us any good, either. I did threaten her, though."

"Oh, good gods, Morgan." Trevor held his hand over his eyes as if he had a headache. Probably he did. I had that effect on people.

"You didn't tell me that," Inigo's voice was very, very calm, but his eyes had turned completely gold.

"Oops." The engines whined, and the plane began to move down the runway.

"Oops? What do you mean, 'oops'?" His eyes were narrowed but I could still see a gold shimmer in the slit between his lids.

"I agree," Trevor said, leaning forward. "What exactly do you mean by 'oops'? You can't just not tell us about these things. Threating the Queen of the Sidhe? That's three steps over into insane."

"Maybe." Couldn't say I entirely disagreed with him. "But she threatened Inigo. She threatened my family. Everyone I love. I am not about to let that happen. She can just back the fuck off. She knows what I can do now, and she knows what'll happen if she messes with any of you."

"Oh, good lord." Trevor sank back in his seat as the plane lifted off.

"What?" I asked.

Inigo sighed and stroked one finger down my cheek. His eyes were back to blue. "That's my girl."

Truly they were annoying me. I proceeded to ignore them for

the next two and a half hours. Unfortunately, once we touched down, I had to go back to being nice to them.

Inigo insisted on staying with the plane.

"Why?" I asked. "Trevor will get you in, just like he did me."

"Uh, not exactly," Trevor admitted.

I stared at him. "Why not?"

"I'm a dragon," Inigo said, as if that explained everything.

"But you don't look like one."

"We've got sensors on base that let us know when a non-human is present. The guards would be on him the minute he stepped inside."

I frowned. "They've never gone off on me."

"You're still human. Mostly."

"Mostly?"

He smiled grimly. "I was able to recalibrate the sensors so they don't detect Atlantean DNA. Otherwise you and I would set them off, too."

Oh, goody.

"I'll be fine, Morgan," Inigo insisted as the pilot brought out a freaking folding lawn chair and set it up in the shade under one of the wings. Where the hell had that been stored? "I'm going to kick back and soak up some sun." He gave me a lazy smile. I was tempted to make a crack about lizards, but instead I gave him a quick peck on the lips before following Trevor across the tarmac. Heat was already shimmering off it in waves, and within three steps I was feeling hot, grumpy, and dehydrated. Even my eyeballs felt shriveled.

As we stepped inside the building that housed the "special" prisoners, I gave a sigh of relief. It was like walking into a refrigeration unit. Now all I needed was some ice cold water, and I'd be good to go.

"Agent Daly. Nice to see you again, sir. Ms. Bailey, ma'am." The guard on duty greeted us with a wide smile across his freckled face.

"Roberts, I thought I told you not to call me ma'am."

"Yes, ma'am. Er, Ms. Bailey. Uh, Morgan." He flushed red and quickly turned to Trevor. "You here to see the colonel, sir?"

"Actually, Roberts, I need to see one of your prisoners. Brent Darroch."

"Oh, of course, sir. I'll take you down." He spoke into his earpiece, and within minutes another guard was taking his place. He was built just like Roberts and had the same earnest expression, only instead of reddish brown hair and freckles, he looked like he'd stepped off the shores of Hawaii and exchanged a surfboard for a 9mm. His black hair was buzzed within an inch of its life, and his dark eyes shone eagerly in his round face. His nametag read Pahia.

Roberts led us through the now familiar gray corridors of Area 51. Somebody had changed the elevator music to what sounded like a Muzak version of one of those hideous children's show theme songs from the '90s. Something with dinosaurs.

"Is that—?"

Roberts grimaced. "Yeah."

"Is it some kind of punishment?"

"Er, one of the guys did it as a joke, and now the colonel is making us listen to it for a month."

"Dear gods."

"Yeah."

Trevor smirked quietly in the corner. Finally the torture ride was over, and Roberts ushered us into the bright, white world of the prison. Darroch was in a different cage from the last time we'd visited, probably because he'd managed to break out of the last one, thanks to Morgana and her magic portals. We'd been assured the new cages were portal- proof. At least until Alister disappeared. Portal-proof, my ass.

We hurried through the airlock and into the inner room that

housed Darroch's cage. Roberts stopped so suddenly, I literally crashed into his back. Trevor stepped on my heel, causing me to wince.

"What's wrong?" he demanded, trying to peer around us.

"Uh, sir. Uh, that, sir." Roberts stepped aside to let us see.

Lying in the middle of the clear glass cage was the huddled form of Brent Darroch. Around him spread a pool of dark red blood.

Chapter 14

"Fuck," Trevor said with feeling.

Roberts said nothing. He marched over and slapped the alarm button near the door. Immediately the wail of sirens echoed through the hallowed halls of Area 51. I grimaced as the sound tortured my already delicate eardrums.

"Can't you shut that thing off in here at least?" I shouted over the wail.

Roberts hit a smaller button, and the siren died, though I could still hear it out in the corridor.

We stared at the scene before us. Arterial spray covered every wall of the eight by ten cage. Whoever killed him had bled him dry.

I stepped closer, eyeing the body through the thick glass. It wasn't glass, of course, but something high tech and unbreakable. Impenetrable. Except something had penetrated it. There were no weapons anywhere inside the cube. I knelt to look at the body. There was so much blood, it was hard to tell, but it looked like he had been stabbed repeatedly.

The door whooshed open and the colonel strode in. I'd met him, but he ignored me, focusing on my brother.

"Report," Trevor ordered.

"Sir," the colonel nodded. "I personally checked the surveillance video."

"And?"

"Nothing. The guard on duty also claims he saw nothing."

"Well, surely you have images of Darroch lying dead."

The colonel shook his head. "No, sir. The video feed shows him alive and well."

"Your video sure is unreliable," I said dryly.

The colonel whirled on me. "Excuse me? I don't think I heard you."

"Oh, you heard me fine," I snapped, straightening. "The last two times people have escaped from this facility, one of them the victim here, your videos have shown nothing. And now you've got a prisoner dead, and yet mysteriously, once again, your surveillance shows nothing."

He stepped closer, his jaw clenched. His face turned beet red all the way up and over his bald head. He puffed out his chest in a clear attempt at intimidation. Asshole obviously thought he was dealing with an ordinary woman. He had no idea I was strong enough to take him out with a single blow. Bastard. "What are you saying, girl?"

"That's Ms. Bailey, to you. *Hunter* if you prefer." I made sure to emphasize my title. You didn't get to be a Hunter for the SRA unless you could kicked some serious ass, and the colonel knew it. "What I'm saying is this is either the most corrupt prison I've ever been in, or the most incompetent."

The colonel grew purple with rage. I could have sworn he was about to hit me. The Darkness inside me laughed, excited by the prospect. Fortunately for him, Trevor stepped in.

"Colonel, I am going to call in my people to do a full audit and inspection of the surveillance systems and the guards. They will also be in charge of the murder investigation. In the meantime, I need access to the cell."

I could have sworn the colonel's face grew even purpler. If he wasn't careful, he was going to keel over from a stroke. He gave a short nod and marched out the door, barking, "Roberts. Let 'em in."

Roberts's freckles stood out even more than usual against his unnaturally pale skin. His eyes were wide as saucers. "Yes, sir!" he shouted after the colonel, then opened the cell for us.

I stepped inside, and that was all I needed. Beneath the copper tang of spilled blood was the scent of greenery and something darker, something rotten. And it didn't come from the body.

"Morgana."

# # #

"You're sure it was the queen?' Trevor asked for what seemed like the thousandth time. I noted he didn't say her name out loud. I was the only one brave or crazy enough to do that.

"Yes, I'm sure," I said, leaning back in my comfy seat. We were on the plane, headed home, and I couldn't get out of Area 51 fast enough. If the SRA didn't replace that colonel fast, I'd be writing a strongly written letter. Or detonating a thermonuclear can of whoop-ass.

Trevor had called his people before we left. I wondered at leaving the colonel running amok without supervision, but Trevor knew what he was doing. I had bigger things to worry about.

I took another deep draft from my ice cold water bottle. I felt drained from the heat of the desert. Even my clothes looked wilted. Trevor, on the other hand, still looked perfectly pressed and polished, as if the heat hadn't affected him in the slightest. As long as he left his sunglasses on so you couldn't see his exhaustion.

"So much for portal-proof prison cells," Inigo said.

I nodded. "Only way to get in there. She is the only one who could have opened the portal. No one else carries quite that stench, and no one else but me, and maybe Emory, can open a portal from the Otherworld anyway. The queen would have to have been really mad to stab him that many times."

"Or just crazy," Trevor pointed out.

"Or both," Inigo chimed in.

"Thank you," I said dryly. "I doubt I could have figured that out on my own."

"Your sarcasm is noted," Trevor said. Inigo grinned at me.

"But why?" I mulled, leaning back to stare at the top of the cabin. "Why would Morgana kill Darroch? Why would she care? She'd already used him for what she needed and thrown him away. He didn't matter anymore. Why go the extra mile?"

"Revenge, maybe?" Trevor suggested.

"What could he have done to piss her off that much? I mean, that's some serious overkill."

"Maybe someone asked her to do it," Inigo suggested.

"I don't know," Trevor said. "It seemed more personal than that. Besides, the queen isn't one to play errand girl."

"Unless Alister and the queen are in on it together," I mused.

"How would that make a difference?"

"Because then the queen likely didn't kill Darroch. She just opened the portal. Alister Jones killed Brent Darroch, and it was very, very personal."

"Shit," Trevor muttered, scrubbing his hands over his face. "Darroch ratted him out to save his own hide. Not to mention his backdoor dealings with the queen."

I nodded. "He tried to snatch the power of the amulet from under Alister's nose. That would have pissed him off big time. Not to mention what he and the queen got up to with Jade."

"But why kill Darroch and not do anything about the queen?"

"Because he can't kill her. She'd be more likely to kill him, and Alister isn't a stupid man. He knows she can be useful to him *if* he can work the right angle on her."

"Alister Jones is a smooth talker," Inigo admitted. "I should know." They were distantly related in a weird, roundabout sort of way. Still, Alister had tried to exterminate the entire dragon race. I wasn't entirely sure he wasn't through with that plan.

"Shit," I said, "We need to find him."

"How?" Trevor asked. "You already looked for him in the

Otherworld, and you can't find him by scrying. Maybe you should focus on this war between the djinn and the Sidhe. Stopping it should be the priority right now."

"It is my priority, but all of this is related somehow. I can feel it in my bones. If we can stop Alister, I think we can stop the war." I shook my head. "Alister has an endgame. And while I still don't know what it is, I know it requires him to be here, in our world. It requires help from the queen. And he needs something else, something he doesn't have yet."

"How do you know that?" Inigo asked.

"Because otherwise he would have already used the grimoire, and we would be dead."

# # #

With no other leads, I decided to call on Cordelia the minute we got back to Portland. Trevor was only marginally mollified by my assurances that stopping Alister would also stop the war, but he returned to the high desert without complaint. When we landed, he'd had a message from Tommy the dome was still holding, but a few cracks were beginning to show.

"How long do you think it will hold?" he'd asked me.

I'd had no idea, of course. This was sort of my first ice dome adventure. Anything could happen. "Just let me know when the cracks get worse. Maybe I can re-ice it." I wasn't at all sure I could do any such thing, but I figured I could give it a shot if I needed to. For now I really needed to find Alister Jones.

"Morgan!" Cordelia threw open the door of her apartment as I raised my fist to knock. "Bastet told me you were on the way. I baked cookies."

"Really?" Cordy had never seemed the cookie-baking type.

She giggled, her cornflower blue eyes sparkling. "Well, I opened a tub of cookie dough, slapped it on a tray, and baked it.

Does that count? They're organic."

"Sure," I said with a grin. "That counts."

"Come on in." She waved me inside. "Have a seat in the living room, and I'll finish the tea." She drifted off down the hall in a swirl of bright red satin. Today's kimono had tiny dragons embroidered all over it.

I edged through a hallway made narrow by ceiling-high bookshelves lined with hardbacks with titles like *The Encyclopedia of Magical Creatures, Poisons from Your Garden,* and *How to Talk to Your Gifted Cat.* There were also plenty of paperbacks sporting images of half-naked men and titles like *For the Love of the Dragon King* and *The Mercenary Playboy's Mistress.* I'd never realized Cordelia had a fondness for romance novels. Something we had in common.

Bastet was in her usual spot among the pillows on the couch. She glared at me through slitted eyes. I liberated a chair from beneath a stack of junk mail, novels, and what looked like ad mock-ups for Cordelia's fortune-telling business, then plopped into it. The cat and I commenced a staring contest.

"Glad to see the two of you getting along," Cordelia chirped as she placed the tea tray on the coffee table, knocking a pile of magazines over in the process. Several of them slithered to the floor. I leaned over to pick them up.

"Oh, don't worry about that." She waved her hand. "I'll get them later." She poured me a cup of tea, plopped a couple of cookies on a plate, and handed it over.

"These smell amazing," I said, trying not to slosh my tea all over them. I'm not a dunker. I preferred my tea and cookies separate. I took a bite and dark chocolate melted across my tongue. "Chocolate chip is my favorite." Okay, oatmeal raisin were my favorite, but people looked at me funny when I said that.

Cordelia snorted. "Liar." I opened my mouth to protest, but

she rattled on. "You wanted to know how to trace Alister Jones."

"Wait. How'd you know that?"

"Bastet, of course."

Of course. "Initially we believed he'd gone to the Otherworld. I think he was there, but we couldn't find a trace of him. Emory, a witch friend of Eddie's, tried scrying for him, but no luck there."

"And Kabita is unaware of his movements."

"Unfortunately, yes. They're not exactly on speaking terms these days."

She nodded. "Well, let us see what the cards have to say." She got up and wandered over to a bookshelf stuffed with crystals, orbs, tarot decks, and other accoutrements of her trade. She walked her fingers along the boxes of tarot decks, at last selecting a brown box. "I think we'll use the steampunk deck this time."

She sat down and pulled the deck from the box, then handed me the cards. I shuffled them and handed them back. We'd done this enough times I knew the routine.

Ignoring her rapidly cooling tea, and the fact that Bastet was eyeing her cookies, Cordy hummed softly to herself as she laid out the cards. "Eight of Wands," she said, laying out the first card. "This means air travel. Lots of action and excitement."

I frowned. "Maybe flying to Area 51? Finding Darroch's body. I wouldn't call it exciting exactly."

"Perhaps. Or perhaps it's something yet to happen." She flipped over the next card. "Five of Cups…interesting. Element of water. Perhaps he is near water?"

"That's clear as mud."

She sighed. "Don't be snarky. The tarot is often vague in such matters. But I've no doubt you will find him when the time is right. The Five of Cups means not all hope is lost. See," she said, tapping the next card with her long, blood-red fingernail. "The chariot. Success!"

"Well, that's good."

"But first…" She flipped the last card. "First you need to turn to your closest friend. That person will have the answer."

"Um, okay." Did she mean Kabita? I mean, Kabita was my best friend, after all.

"Yes, Kabita."

"Excuse me?" I hadn't said anything aloud.

"Bastet agrees with you. You need to talk with Kabita. She will be able to steer you in the right direction. But first finish your cookies."

Like I needed urging to do that.

Chapter 15

"How did the demon hunt go?" I asked when Kabita answered her phone.

"You know," she replied. "Same old, same old. I hunt demon, I kill demon, I go home to wash off the demon goo."

"Sounds like fun." I unlocked my car and climbed into the passenger seat. Bastet was in the window staring down at me. I stuck my tongue out at her. I could have sworn she sneered back. "Hey, what do you know about portals?"

"Excuse me?"

"You know, portals. Little wormholes or whatever to and from the Otherworld."

"Why do you need to know about portals?"

"Um, your dad might've escaped the Otherworld through one."

"Shit."

I always knew things were bad when Kabita started swearing. She wasn't wrong. Things were definitely bad.

"Here's what we know. He definitely escaped Area 51 through a portal to the Otherworld. We also know he's in cahoots with the queen, though we don't know why. We also know he got into Darroch's cell using a portal from the Otherworld which the queen probably opened, and all that's left of Darroch is a big blood puddle on the floor. Scrying for Alister's location didn't work, and I'm pretty sure he didn't stay in the Otherworld for long."

"Why do you think that?"

"Because he's got shit to do. And whatever it is, I'm convinced it doesn't involve the Otherworld. Your dad is a "for the humans" guy."

"True."

"I wish there was some way to trace him through the portal.

I mean, we know he came through from the Otherworld and no doubt went back the same way. And he had to have used one to travel from the Otherworld to wherever he is now."

"Double shit."

"You're telling me. Unfortunately, we haven't been able to trace Alister since. I think possibly the queen is hiding him or something. He has to be somewhere here on Earth."

"And you want to try to trace him through the portals." It wasn't a question.

"I know it sounds crazy," I said, "but it's the only thing I can think of. Like I said, Emory tried to scry for him but it didn't work."

"Of course not," Kabita said. "My father is far too sneaky for that sort of thing."

"So the portal," I prompted. "Is it possible? Can we trace him?"

She sighed. "Once the portal is closed, other than being able to trace its origins, it's pretty much impossible."

"Shit." Great. Now I was the one cussing. Because that was so unusual.

"What we can do," Kabita said, "is trace his signature through the portal system."

I paused, leaning back in my seat. Bastet was still staring at me. "There is a portal system? Like, a highway system?"

"Sort of."

"Why didn't I know this?" I had been a Hunter for three years. No, make that nearly four. This was the first time I'd heard about a portal system. What else was she hiding from me?

"It's not something we talk about."

"Who do you mean, we? The guardians of the portals?" Okay, so I was being a little snarky. I couldn't help myself. People keeping things from me tended to make me really mad. And yes, I got the irony.

"No," Kabita said slowly. "I'm talking about witches."

"Excuse me?"

She sighed again. "It's a long story. Let's just say a long time ago in a galaxy right here where we stand, a coven of witches took a vow to protect the portals. It's been our job ever since."

"So how did the Queen of the Sidhe get her hands on a portal?"

"She's not human. She creates her own portals. She doesn't need to use the portal ways like we do."

Possibilities whirled through my head. The portal system could be the answer to fast travel and better hunting. And what about other planets? Did the portals go to other planets or just Earth? Clearly they went to other dimensions... I shook my head. I needed to focus. "So how are we going to track Alister? If he's not using the regular portal ways?"

"Even though she creates her own portals, the queen still leaves a trace within the system. Those of us with witch blood can sense those traces sometimes."

"This sounds like a really long story," I said.

"You have no idea."

I desperately wanted to hear it, but we had more important things to deal with. I could find out more after we captured Alister and got back the grimoire. "Fine. What do we need to do right now in order to trace him?"

"We wait until the full moon."

"Figures."

I stood at the edge of a lake, the water lapping the rock-strewn shore. I knew it was a lake because there was no salt tang in the air, but the water was so vast it seemed like an ocean. I could not see the end of it, only the infinite water stretching toward the horizon.

All around the lake, tall evergreen trees towered high into the blue sky. Long grasses waved in the gentle breeze making a faint hushing sound. It was a warm day, and small bees buzzed about tiny flowers hidden in the grass. A butterfly flitted inches from my face, its blue wings stretched out in the sun. I drew in a deep breath. All I smelled was the fresh perfume of a summer day. Not a speck of smog to pollute the air. I wiped a bead of sweat from my upper lip and worried vaguely about the burn of sun on my back. I should probably seek the shade soon.

The grating sound of metal against metal reached my ears. I turned to look behind me. Several women dressed in leather leggings, breasts bound, were setting up a small camp, erecting tents and building a fire. I recognized them instantly. They were from my previous dreams of the princess of Atlantis, the women who protected her for centuries. The Amazons. But this wasn't the Old World, not Europe where they'd originally made their home. This was someplace new, someplace different. I'd seen it in my most recent dream vision. This was the place where the Amazons had been attacked. This place was in the New World.

I walked toward the camp to help but was intercepted by a tall woman with long dark hair tied up in a knot. One side of her face was covered in tattoos. More tattoos twisted down her arms. Like the others, she wore a binding across her breasts and tight buckskin breeches. A quiver of arrows was on her back, and she held a bow in one hand. A short sword, like something a Roman centurion might use, was strapped against her side, and a hunting knife was on her thigh.

"Princess," she said, inclining her head slightly. "You seem far away."

"I miss our home." The voice that spoke was not my own, nor were the words.

"You know it became too dangerous to remain there." She tapped the tip of her bow against her thigh. "We had no choice. We had to leave or risk losing everything."

"I understand," I said. "But why this place? So far away from everything we know. So empty."

She stared across the water, her expression far away. "It was part of

Amaza's plan. The one handed down through the generations. They say that long ago, before Atlantis fell, it established colonies in the far reaches of this planet. When Atlantis fell, so did the colonies. Only one survived the scourge. An outpost on the shores of this lake."

I was startled. "Here? But why?"

"Copper, she said. "They harvested metals from this area. It's rich in them. They shipped them back to Atlantis. There was a plan to build a city here eventually. I was hoping there would be someone left. Someone who could keep you safe."

"You mean you were hoping there were some Atlanteans left," I said. "That we weren't the last."

She nodded. "I'd hoped so."

"But we haven't seen anyone," I said. "Not even a sign there was ever anything here."

She nodded thoughtfully. "I don't believe we have found the last colony as yet. We must keep looking. Otherwise all will be lost."

"And if we don't find the colony?" I asked.

"Then there is only one other option open to us."

My heart filled with a dread I didn't understand.

Chapter 16

I opened my eyes to sun streaming into my room. I had forgotten to close the blackout curtains. I squinted at my alarm clock. Far too early.

Inigo was curled up next to me, one arm draped across my waist. I would've liked to stay in bed all day. The thought definitely had merit. But we had things to do. Alister was still loose with the grimoire, there was a war going on, and I needed to decide what to do next.

Since we were forced to wait for the full moon, which was several days away, I decided it was time to talk to my mom about Michigan. I'd recognized the lake in my dream. It was a place I'd dreamt about before. It was one of the Great Lakes. I was sure of it, but what that had to do with Alister or my father I had no idea. I rolled out of bed and padded to the shower. As I stood under the hot spray, I replayed the dream in my mind. I wasn't sure which lake it was—hard to tell from a dream— but I was certain it was in Michigan. The state had come up too often to ignore.

It made sense that Alister and my father would be interested in Michigan if that really was the location of the last colony of Atlantis. But what did that have to do with the grimoire? And what did any of it have to do with the Queen of the Sidhe? How would the grimoire and Michigan and all of this other stuff help her win the war against the djinn? And what did Alister have up his sleeve? What was his big plan?

As I dried off, I told myself to stop freaking out. If I didn't stop running this through my mind I was gonna go crazy. I wouldn't know what Alister was up to until I found him, and I wouldn't be able to find him until Kabita traced the portal system. Other than the whole last colony of Atlantis possibly being in Michigan thing, I wouldn't know what it had to do with anything until I talked to my mom. If she even knew anything.

I slapped on some makeup, did a quick blow-dry of my hair, and then slipped back into the bedroom. I thought I was being quiet while rummaging for something in the closet, but apparently, I wasn't quiet enough for dragon hearing. Inigo rolled over in bed.

"Hey, gorgeous," he said. His voice was a sleepy rumble. I turned to stare at him lying there all delicious and rumpled. There was nothing more I wanted than to climb back into bed with him and forget about this whole stupid thing. But I was a Hunter. I didn't get to climb under the covers and pretend bad things weren't happening.

"Hey, yourself," I said, giving him what I hoped was a seductive smile. "You gonna lay in bed all day, or are you gonna visit my mother with me?"

"Oh gee. Now there is a hard choice," he said dryly, sitting up. The covers drooped to reveal a tantalizing amount of naked male flesh. My mouth went a little dry.

I snatched his T-shirt off the floor and threw it at his head. "Don't be ridiculous. I need to talk to my mother about Michigan."

"Michigan?"

I'd forgotten that whole Michigan thing had come up while he'd been recovering in dragon territory. "You've kind of missed a lot," I said.

He stared at me for a moment, face expressionless. "Yeah. I get that." His voice was very quiet. Very grim.

I strode over to sit by him. I ran my fingers through the silky blond hair. I'd missed him so much, my heart ached with it. "I didn't mean it like that. Not having you here was one of the hardest things ever. It was worse than dying." And I should know, having truly died. "I've just... I'm so used to always having you here. You were always there for me, always. And suddenly you were gone. Emotionally, I felt lost. So much happened while you were away, and I had to keep going. I didn't have a choice."

Inigo wrapped his arms around me, pulling me hard against him. He was so warm, and I could hear the throb of his heart against my ear. This. I'd missed this.

"I'm sorry," he said. "So sorry."

"It wasn't all your fault."

"Part of it, no," he agreed, "but I chose to stay away when I could've been with you. You were right about that. And for that I am sorry."

"I get it. You had things to work through. I've been there. I know exactly what you're going through. And I didn't have anybody except Kabita, and while we're best friends now, back then she wasn't even sure she was going to let me live. So yeah, I get it. And I wish, I wish so much you would've let me help you. Let me go through it with you. Because I could've handled it. But I don't blame you because I understand that sometimes, some things you just have to go through on your own."

His arms tightened around me, and he kissed my forehead. "I love you, Morgan Bailey," he said. "More than you can ever possibly know."

I leaned back and stared up into his beautiful blue eyes. "I don't know about that. But I love you too."

He kissed me then, and I felt it all the way to my toes. We ended up being a lot later than I planned to get to my mother's.

# # #

My mother practically rolled out the red carpet the minute she saw Inigo. While she'd never been a fan of Jack's, Inigo was one of her favorite people ever. I'm pretty sure she liked him more that she liked me, her own daughter.

"Oh, you sweet boy," she exclaimed drawing him into the house. "I haven't seen you in ages. How have you been?" She was perfectly coiffed, as usual, her hair carefully pinned in a French twist. Her pearls were impeccably straight, and her black slacks immaculately pressed. She looked like she was trying out for some kind of '50s housewife movie role, except they would have never worn pants.

"Good to see you, Mrs. B," Inigo said, kissing her on the cheek. I noticed he avoided the question of how he'd been. Good thing. I could just imagine my mother's reaction if he told her he'd almost died. Or did die. Or whatever happened. I was still a little fuzzy on the details, and the dragons weren't sharing. Anyway, most things were better if my mother didn't know, especially when it came to the paranormal.

"Come right into the kitchen," she said hurrying us along. "I just finished baking snicker doodles."

That explained the gorgeous scent of vanilla and cinnamon that wafted out of the kitchen. Although not my favorite cookie, they were certainly up there in the get-in-my-tummy-now department. It also hadn't gone unnoticed that my mother hadn't even bothered to greet me.

"Hello to you too, mother," I mumbled.

"Morgan, muttering is in no way ladylike." She didn't even turn to look at me. I swear the woman had bionic ears. I didn't bother pointing out that no one in their right mind considered me a lady unless they wanted to lose a body part.

In the kitchen, Mother sat us down with a plate of cookies and glasses of milk like we were ten years old. Inigo, grinning like a lunatic, crammed an entire cookie in his mouth. Such behavior would've gotten me a lecture fifteen minutes long, but Mother smiled and patted Inigo on the head like he was the cutest thing she'd ever seen while he got crumbs all over her pristine table. I rolled my eyes.

"That's enough from you, young lady."

How did she do that? She wasn't looking at me.

"Mom," I said, "we're not here for just a visit."

"I didn't think you were," she said tartly. "You never visit unless you need something."

"That's not true," I said although I had to admit I couldn't remember the last time I'd visited her when I didn't need something. Oh yeah, my birthday. When was that? Six months ago? Seven?

"What is it you need this time?" She sat down at the table and folded her hands primly. She didn't bother taking a cookie, nor did she pour a drink for herself.

"Okay," I said, diving right in, "have you ever heard of Michigan?"

She looked at me like I'd grown a second head. "Of course I've heard of Michigan. Who hasn't? Didn't you learn about these things in school? Why did I pay so much for your education?"

Refraining from rolling my eyes again, I continued, "No, I mean did you ever hear Dad talk about Michigan? Or maybe Alister?"

Her expression grew tight. My mother really didn't like talking about my father or Alister Jones. She'd spent most of my life telling me my father left us when the truth was he died. She'd refused to tell me anything about him, allowing me to believe he was some sort of douchebag who'd deserted his family. My mother was truly the queen of avoidance.

"I don't see why this is important," she said stiffly. Her hand drifted up to twist her pearls, a sure sign she was distressed.

"Trust me, Mom, it is. Did Dad ever mention Michigan? Or anything related to Michigan? A lake, maybe."

She stared at the clock on the wall so long I thought she wasn't going to answer. "Not that I recall," she finally said. I

114

honestly wasn't sure if she was telling the truth or not. My mother had a way of lying to herself so well even she believed it.

"And Alister Jones? Did he ever mention anything about it?"

"Why would I know anything about what Alister Jones knew or didn't know about Michigan?"

"Mom, don't be like that...."

"Be like what?" she snapped. "I really don't see why these questions are important. This is all in the past. I've had nothing to do with that man in years."

"Trust me, Mom, it's important. Please. Did Alister ever mention Michigan?"

She actually seemed to give it some thought. "There was this one time...."

Inigo and I leaned forward eagerly. "Yes?" Inigo prompted her.

She gave Inigo a smile a little bit warmer than the one she'd given me. "It was shortly before your father... left." Clearly she still couldn't admit my father hadn't had a choice. I reined in my anger and nodded. She continued. "I overheard them talking about a lakeshore in Michigan. I assumed they wanted to go fishing or something. Although it was strange because your father wasn't one for fishing. The minute I entered the room, they stopped talking about it and started behaving very strangely."

"What you mean by strangely?" I asked.

She sighed. "I don't know. Your father rarely kept secrets from me in those days, but he didn't seem to want me to know about their discussion. I suppose that's why it stuck in my mind. That, and the fact it was Michigan. We didn't know anyone in Michigan."

"Did they say anything more specific?" Inigo asked.

"Not that I recall." Her tone was firm. I knew we'd get nothing more out of her.

But Inigo was not about to give up. "Do you happen to have any books or papers that belonged to Alexander Morgan?" he asked.

"Actually I do," she said.

I stared at her with my mouth open. I couldn't believe my ears. My whole life I'd been asking about things that belonged to my father, and she'd always denied me, claiming everything was destroyed. Now she was saying she had some of his things?

I started to open my mouth when Inigo interrupted me with a look. Clearly he knew me far too well. "Can we see them?" he asked.

She gave him a long look. "This way."

She led us into the small den just off the kitchen and pushed open a narrow door that led into a storage closet. At the back was a rickety old bookshelf I remembered well from my childhood. It was crammed with old copies of National Geographic, dusty tomes of folklore, and a few cheap paperbacks. Although I'd loved pouring over the books as a child, my mother had often shooed me away when she saw me going through the shelves. Eventually she started locking the closet so I couldn't get in. After a while, I forgot about it, new interests taking me elsewhere.

"Everything on that bookcase belonged to Alex," Mom said softly but with little emotion. "If there was anything, it would be there."

"You mind if we go through it?" Inigo asked gently.

She shrugged. There was tightness around her eyes that hadn't been there before. "Suit yourself," she said. And then she turned and walked away.

Chapter 17

I heaved a sigh. I got it. I did. My mother had experienced so much pain, thanks to my father and Alister, it was a wonder she could have any normal life at all. I just hated that I was the one left dealing with this frigid woman who refused to face the truth.

I shook off the maudlin thoughts and turned my attention to the bookshelf. My father's books. How had I never known? I skimmed my fingers along the dusty spines. The books that had always fascinated me were suddenly fraught with meaning.

"You take that end," Inigo said, nodding at the left side of the bookshelf. "And I'll take this end. What are we looking for?"

"Any books pertaining to Michigan," I said. "Plus anything that looks like an important document, personal letter, anything that might give us a clue as to what Alister is up to, where he's gone, or why Michigan is so important."

Inigo nodded and we began digging through the books. Dust *poofe*d up in small clouds, making me sneeze. Inigo rubbed his nose as if the dust tickled him too.

"Don't you dare sneeze in here," I said. "I do not want these books going up in flames."

He laughed. "You know very well I don't breathe fire in human form."

I grinned. It felt so good to have him at my side again, fighting the bad guys and what not. I'd missed that so much. "Yeah, I know. I just don't want you to forget."

He leaned over, grabbed the back of the head, and pressed a kiss to my mouth. It was hard and fast and hot as hell. Heat pooled low in my belly and all I could think about was losing myself in him.

"Don't distract me," I said a little breathlessly as I pulled away. "I need to focus."

Inigo winked and went back to pawing through the rows of books.

About a half an hour later, I was covered in dust and grime and was no closer to learning the truth. My gritty eyes burned and my sinuses felt like they had cotton stuffed up in them. I let out about the sixth sneeze. I was itchy everywhere thanks to the dust.

I reached for particularly thick book on human anatomy. Seemed an odd sort of tome for my father to have. It wasn't like he'd been a doctor or anything. I flipped through the pages not expecting to find anything. An envelope fell out. It was thick and had several pages inside, yellowed with age. I pulled them out and unfolded them carefully.

"What's that you've got there?" Inigo asked, leaning closer.

"I'm not sure."

"It looks like a deed." He squinted at the tiny writing on the page.

"You mean like to a house or something?" I asked, handing it to him. "Maybe it's my mom's."

He nodded. "Except this isn't to her house. It looks like it involves a plot of land, and it's in your father's name."

I'd never heard of my father owning any land. Certainly nothing that would've passed to my mother, as she wasn't technically his next of kin. "Probably something Trevor and his mom inherited when he died," I said.

"I don't think so," Inigo said. "It's in your name, too."

"What?" I said, grabbing the documents from his hand. "How is that possible? I wasn't even born when my father died."

"And yet, here it is. Your name. Maybe your parents had picked out a name before you were born."

I doubted that, but it was possible. "What kind of property?"

"It looks like undeveloped land."

"Where?" I skimmed the document but s so much legal

jargon put my mind in a tumble, and everything kind of melted together. I realized I was shaking.

He gently took it back from me and scanned the pages. "It looks like…" He grinned. "It's near Lake Superior. Michigan."

# # #

I had more than a sneaking suspicion that the deed was closely related to whatever was going on with Alister. My father and Alister had once been best friends. It wasn't out of the realm of possibility that Alister would know the location of the property my father had purchased in Michigan. But why? Why would my father buy some random piece of land in a state he had no connection to whatsoever? And then put my name on the deed? What was it about this place that he and Alister were so obsessed over? Could it be that he, too, knew about the last colony of Atlantis? And could the property have something to do with that?

So many questions and absolutely no answers. My mother claimed to know nothing of the property, either, nor that the deed was on the bookshelf. She seemed confused about my name being on the deed, insisting they had never decided on a name for me. I had to take her word for it. But that left me with even more questions. Maybe Tommy would know something. But then why wouldn't Tommy have told me? Or Trevor?

With both Tommy and Trevor busy with the war, and the full moon rapidly approaching, I decided the best thing to do was focus on our next task: scanning the portals. I needed more information. If there was one man who would know more about this portal business, it was Eddie Mulligan.

The next day I left Inigo snoring in bed and headed down to Majicks and Potions, Eddie's New Age shop over on Hawthorne Street. As I entered the shop, the bell above the door jangled, and I almost choked on a cloud of incense.

Eddie beamed at me from behind the register. He was perched on a high stool, glasses propped on the end of his nose, book in hand. The cover was of a very scantily clad woman armed with what looked like a whip. I nearly blushed.

"Do you like it?" he asked.

I blinked. "Um…." The woman's nearly bare ass stared back at me.

"It's new. Elysian Fields, they call it."

Oh. Right. The incense. "It's rather…strong," I said, waving it away from my face.

He sighed. "Yes. It would have been a great option for covering up the ganja. But that no longer matters." With the legalization of recreational marijuana in the state of Oregon, users wouldn't have to cover up the scent anymore. Not that incense had ever really worked, to be honest. Too bad for Eddie and his wonderful new incense. "But I don't suppose you came to talk about my sales woes," he said, laying the book down on the counter.

"Nope. I've got some questions about portals."

"Oh, portals." He beamed. "That's exciting. Have you been portal traveling again lately?"

"In fact, I have." I quickly told him about my trip to the Otherworld, make that "trips" plural, and about Alister's escape from prison, along with our less than fruitful attempts to find him. "Kabita thinks she might be able to track him through what she called the portal system, and Cordelia agreed, although neither of them would tell me much about it. Have you ever heard of this system?"

His eyes widened. "But of course. Although the system hasn't been used much in centuries."

"You mean other than by the Queen of the Sidhe."

"Well, yes, her. Although she doesn't technically use the

system itself. She creates her own portals."

"Yeah," I said. "Kabita told me that. But I want to know more about the system. How does it work? Why are the witches in charge of it? How come I've never heard of it before?"

He laughed. "So many questions. Let me start with the first. I honestly have no idea how it works."

I stared at him for a moment. Today he was wearing red corduroy pants paired with an evergreen-colored button-down shirt. Over the top of that was a navy and white striped waistcoat and a gold bowtie. His usual blinding ensemble.

I glanced around the shop to make sure we were alone. "But you are a Titan," I said in a low voice. "Isn't that like one of the basic tenets of the universe that you're supposed to know?"

"But I'm not all-knowing," he said with a smile. "I've kind of been out of top slot with most of the universe for the last few millennia. My best guess is that it has something to do with wormholes and alternate dimensions. But that's way beyond my pay grade."

I wondered what pay grade you had to be in order to be privy to this sort of information. Being a Titan was kind of like being a god. In fact being a Titan technically made Eddie older than the gods.

"Okay, so forget the technicalities. How does it work for travel?"

He pondered that for a moment. "Let's get the book out, shall we?"

Eddie reached below the counter and pulled out a massive book wrapped in ancient silk. Removing the covering carefully, he placed the book on the counter. The cover was made of thick leather polished to a high sheen. Embossed on the front was a simple representation of the Tree of Life. It was a surprisingly plain looking thing for what it was. Eddie flipped open the cover.

"Please illustrate the portal system." He enunciated each word precisely. At first nothing happened. Then the pages began to turn on their own, finally stopping about halfway through.

"Don't you love having a sentient book?" Eddie rubbed his hands together with glee. "Look at that."

I looked. The page contained an elaborate drawing in rich hues of blue, green, and gold. It seemed to illustrate some kind of tunnel-like system of doorways. The tunnels branched out in crazy patterns with archways opening into what appeared to be various locations. Swirling words littered the pages, apparently describing the illustrations. It looked surprisingly like a simplified version of the London Tube map, only instead of names like "Cockfosters" and "Chorleywood," the labels read "Tenth Level of Hell" and "Los Angeles Central."

"You know how the portal to the Otherworld operates, yes?" Eddie asked.

"Of course," I said. "The queen creates the portal, you step through, and you arrive on the other side. Oh, and you feel like puking when you get there."

Eddie slapped his knees and laughed so hard his belly shook. "Oh my, yes. That's exactly how it feels."

"You've traveled through it before?" I asked.

"Once. Very long ago. All portals essentially work the same way." He placed his finger on one of the illustrations. The doorway opened onto what looked like the Giza Plateau. "They all exist in time and space, but like the djinn, they can be out of phase with our reality. It takes someone with very strong magic to bring the portal entrance into our world so we can use it."

Okay," I said with a nod. "I get that. Kabita seemed to think all the portals were connected."

He traced the line of tunnel things with his finger. "Exactly so. Think of it like a network of tunnels. Only instead of running underground, they run through time and space between different dimensions. And instead of manhole covers leading up onto the street, they use portals that will spill you out into one place or another."

It made perfect sense. The book's illustration showed it clearly. "All right, so how come I've never heard of this before?"

"Well, like I said, it takes an extremely strong magical practitioner to open the portals. There aren't many of those around anymore and there haven't been for several hundred years. No magic workers, no portal travel. It sort of fell out of vogue, if you will, what with modern transportation."

Other than the puking part, I still thought portals were a quicker and better mode of travel, and a lot easier to carry weapons through. TSA sort of frowned on that. "Seems like the portals would be a lot safer than airplanes."

"You'd think so."

I waited.

"The odds of getting run through, blown up, or eaten by hostiles upon exiting the system are approximate one in ten thousand."

"Seems like pretty good odds to me," I said, somewhat relieved.

"The chances of dying in a plane crash are one in eleven million."

There went that idea. "All right, but what about the witches? Why are they in charge?"

"Back when the portals were being used on a regular basis, the powers that be felt it was important to put control of the portals into the hands of someone who wouldn't be easily swayed or corrupted by power."

"The powers that be?"

"Trust me, you don't want to know."

I took his word for it. "So, these powers, they chose witches."

"Not just any witches," he said. "A very special coven of witches. A genetic bloodline that has existed for centuries, since the dawn of humanity."

"Since the Atlanteans came?" I guessed.

His smile was slow and sly. "As you say."

Suddenly it was all coming together. The ancient bloodline of witches, the portal system, Alister, Michigan, and the grimoire. I'd bet my last dollar that this witch coven, the one that was in charge of the portal system, also was needed for whatever spell was in that grimoire. Which meant Alister would need them too. Fortunately, I'd got to them first. Because I now knew Emory was one of those witches.

"Thanks, Eddie," I said turning toward the door," that's a big help."

"Where are you off to?" he asked.

"I'm off to find me a witch."

Chapter 18

I watched the moon slide up through the velvet black sky. Round and full, glowing with pure, white light. I closed my eyes, took a deep breath, and drank in the darkness around me. The Darkness within me stirred, drawing energy from the night. It was both my blessing and my curse. A creature who drew energy not from the sun or from blood, but from the shadows. That which had been mankind's natural enemy for centuries, the thing we feared to our very bones, the place where the nightmares hid was the place from where I drew my strength. Talk about fucked up.

We were in Emory's backyard, the overgrown bushes and witch wards providing protection from prying eyes. Emory and her coven sisters were setting out candles. I wondered if all of them were the descendants of the coven Eddie had told me about. I was certain Emory was but not so sure about the others.

Since Emory's coven consisted of only herself and two others, Kabita and Cordelia were joining them for the evening to make up the four elements so Emory could take the center. Although not technically a witch, Kabita had insisted Cordy had enough magic to do what needed doing. Although traditionally a coven of witches was thirteen, three was sufficient. Four was best for calling the corners, or so Kabita had told me. Five was even better. I'd take better.

It was all women tonight. Kabita had told me male energies would muck with the female energy of the full moon. I had no idea what that had to do with the portals and Alister, but I was going with it.

One of the witches approached me, a silver bowl in her hands. She held it out to me like an offering, a slight smile curving her full lips. Her dark, curly hair fell midway down her back, its true color unrecognizable in the darkness. Her skin was dusky in the moonlight, her eyes no more than pools of black. Even my night vision wasn't that good.

"Here," she said. "You will need this later in the ritual."

"Oh, I'm not part of the ritual."

Her smile widened. "Sure you are."

"No, seriously I'm not. I'm just here for information. I'm not a witch." And I really wanted nothing to do with the portals. The queen's portal was enough for me.

She gazed at me for a long time. I tried to remember her name. Something exotic. It just wouldn't come to me. Finally she spoke.

"Everyone here tonight, everyone who seeks knowledge, must participate in the ritual. Must be bound by the ritual." She gave me a look that told me there was a great deal of meaning to her word choice. Especially the "bound" part. The idea didn't sit well with me.

"I have no magic." It was the truth as far as it went. I had tons of magic, it just wasn't the kind necessary for tonight's little shindig.

She tilted her head to one side and eyed me much like a cat might eye a tasty bird. She laid one hand on my arm, her dusky skin a sharp contrast to the glowing alabaster of my own. "Oh yes," she said slowly. "You have a great deal of magic."

Wonderful. She could sense the powers inside me. Not exactly my idea of a plus. "I'm not a witch. I don't have witch magic."

"Nor does your friend, Cordelia, and yet she is willing to lend us what she does have. For the greater good."

I felt guilty, which pissed me off. "I know nothing about the portals."

"And yet you called one."

I stared at her for a moment. "How did you know that?

Sorry, what was your name?"

She didn't bat an eyelash. "Veronique. But my friends call me Veri. As to how I knew about the portal, we all know about the portal."

Fantastic. Now I had a coven of witches poking their noses in my business. Just what I needed.

"Fine. Veri." I took the bowl. Inside was some kind of goop I didn't want to name. "But if this goes wrong, don't blame me."

She laughed lightly and padded barefoot across the grass to where the circle would be. She glanced over her shoulder. "You better hope nothing goes wrong."

Was that a threat? I wasn't sure if I liked this Veri person or not. Unlike Emory, there was a shrewdness about her which made me uncomfortable. And yet Emory had chosen her as part of the coven, so she couldn't be that bad. Right? However, she was definitely hiding something.

I shook my head. Not my monkeys, not my circus. I had bigger things to worry about than coven politics. I needed information, and if Veronique was one of the people I needed to help me get it, then I would damn well use her.

"We're ready," Emory called.

I walked over to join them. Cordelia, Veronique, Kabita, and the other witch, Lene, stood at the four corners of the circle. Each one held a white unlit candle in her hand. They were barefoot, their toes curled in the cool grass, and wore flowing white gowns reminiscent of something from a painting of fairies. Even Kabita had shed her usual skintight black jeans for a dress. Frankly, it was a little bizarre seeing her decked out that way.

Emory made me stand in the middle of the circle with my bowl. Beneath my hands was a small brazier on a tripod. Inside glowed several coals which Emory had taken from the fire pit. The warmth radiated on the back of my hands and my jean-clad shins.

Satisfied I was in exactly the right spot, Emory began to walk the circle, chanting while she drew a thin line of salt. The others remained in their positions, silent. Once the circle was drawn, Emory commenced with the calling of the four corners. She paced toward Veri, stopping in front of her.

"Hail to the Guardians of the Watchtowers of the East, powers of air and creation. Hear Me!"

Veri's candlewick burst into flame. Emory stepped to her right, stopping in front of Lene.

"Hail to the Guardians of the Watchtowers of the South, powers of fire and emotion. Hear Me!"

Lene's candle caught flame, picking out the golden highlights in her hair. She smiled at Emory as if a magically lit candle was just the best thing ever. Emory walked over to Cordelia, who was looking a little nervous

"Hail to the Guardians of the Watchtowers of the West, powers of water and awareness. Hear Me!"

Cordy looked a little worried when her candle lit, but she held steady. I grinned at her, and she seemed to relax.

Kabita was next.

"Hail to the Guardians of the Watchtowers of the North, powers of mother and earth. Hear Me!"

Huh. I hadn't associated Kabita with anything motherly, although she was awfully bossy. Still, the candle cupped in her hands burst into flame.

I expected them to put their candles down and do something interesting, but they remained where they were, me in the center with my bowl, them at the four corners with their candles. Emory paced slowly toward me, something grasped in the palm of her hand. She stopped directly across the brazier from me, and let whatever was in her hands drop onto the hot coals. There was a small burst of flame, and a cloud of pungent smoke. Herbs of some kind, I guessed. I coughed and tried to wave the worst of the smoke away.

With all four flames burning and the brazier smoking away, they began to chant in unison. Unlike the other times I'd seen Emory cast a spell, they spoke English.

"By the night in his soul, I call darkness to guide me so Alister Jones must be found. By beat of his heart, I call instinct to guide me so Alister must be found. By the voice of his spirit, I call knowledge to guide me so Alister must be found. By the gods he hath angered, I call you to guide me so Alister must be found. By the portals of time, I call you to guide me so Alister will be found."

As they spoke the last word, the contents of the bowl began to change color. The dark muck morphed into a shimmering silver reminiscent of the portal entrances I'd seen. I stared into the bowl, surprised. Was I supposed to see something? Because there was nothing there but my reflection staring back at me from the silver.

"Look into the bowl and ask your question," Emory ordered.

I felt weird doing it, but I stared into that strange liquid and asked my question. "Where is Alister Jones?"

Nothing happened. I glanced up at Emory, who shook her head. "You must be more specific. It can't show you what it can't see."

I guess that meant Alister wasn't currently in the portal system. "Show me where Alister Jones has been."

The silver muck shifted, and within it shapes began to coalesce. First, there was a clear picture of Alister Jones striding into a portal opening. Behind him was what looked like Brent Darroch's room at Area 51. Clearly, this was where Alister had entered the actual portal system rather than the queen's Otherworld portal.

He strode through tunnel after tunnel of the system. The

tunnel walls were a sort of cloudy bluish-white. They shifted and stirred like one would expect clouds to do. Sometimes it seemed lightning flashed along the walls. It was eerie to say the least. Alister seemed surprisingly comfortable, as if he'd walked these tunnels before.

He approached a branch and went right. In front of him another portal opened, and he stepped out. Before the portal closed behind him, cutting off my view, I caught a glimpse of the landscape. Tall trees, waving grasses, and water so vast it looked like an ocean. I opened my eyes. It was the lake from my dreams. Alister was in Michigan.

# # #

I tried calling Tommy once again before Emory opened the portal for me. I needed to know about Michigan before I left, but I had to move quickly. Gods only knew what Alister was up to. Whatever it was, it could only spell disaster.

I couldn't get a hold of Tommy, but I managed to reach Trevor. He sounded out of breath.

"Make it quick," he snapped. "The ice has cracked completely. Chunks of the dome are down, and I'm not sure how much longer we can hold them."

"Why didn't you tell me?" I snapped. "I told you to let me know if anything happened. I might have been able to repair it."

"Too late. There goes another section."

"Okay, I'm on my way," I said grimly.

"You'll never get here in time."

He was right, of course. By car, even driving like a bat out of hell, it would take nearly three hours to get to Tommy's. "I've got something special in mind."

"Make it snappy." He disconnected.

"Emory, forget Michigan. I need you to open a portal to

djinn lands. Can you do it?"

"I can open the portal system. That's easy enough. But once you're in, you're the one who has to navigate. Without the coordinates, you could be lost forever."

Freaking fantastic. "How do we get coordinates? Can you find them on a map? What?"

"It would help if there was a witch at the other end."

"Well, there isn't." A thought struck me. "But there's Tommy. He's a shaman. Would that work?"

She mulled it over. "It might. Veri?"

Veri nodded. "I need a map."

I pulled out my smartphone and opened the map application. "This work?"

"Sure. Can you show me where djinn lands are approximately?"

I zoomed into Central Oregon and the Warm Springs Reservation. "About here."

"And this Tommy is a shaman? One to whom you have a personal connection?"

I nodded. "Yeah. He's sort of my mentor."

"Even better. Give me your hand."

I frowned but held up my hand. She took it, and with my phone in one hand and my hand in the other, she closed her eyes and made a humming sound. I gazed over her head at Emory, who nodded encouragingly. I shrugged and stayed where I was though it felt awkward as hell.

Finally Emory stopped humming. "Got it. There's a portal not far from where the shaman is. I need a pencil and some paper."

Lene appeared at her side with an old envelope and a stub of a pencil. Veri finally let go of my hand and gave me back my cell phone. She quickly sketched a map on the envelope. "Follow this exactly. Deviate even a little, and we might not get you back.

Understand?"

"Got it." I took the envelope and stared at it. It looked simple enough.

"All right, let's open this portal," Emory said. "Everyone stand back."

Unlike the Otherworld portal, she didn't draw a circle, use herbs, or even chant. She just muttered a couple words, raised her hands, palm outward, and a portal shimmered into existence.

"Remember," Veri said, grabbing my arm. "Follow the directions exactly."

I nodded and stepped through the portal, Kabita hot on my heels. The portal sealed shut behind us.

We were inside a tunnel which was about a foot taller than me, with sides far enough apart to give us room to walk side by side. The walls swirled in blues and whites like clouds shifting through the summer sky. Lightning jagged across ceiling and floor accompanied not by the crash of thunder, but by an odd sizzling sound. Otherwise the tunnels were eerily silent. We walked straight ahead. There was nowhere else to go.

"Now where?" Kabita whispered. We'd come to a three-way branch. I studied the map carefully.

"Keep going straight," I answered in the same hushed tone. There was something about the silence that made me feel like I was inside a library or something. The need to whisper was too compelling to ignore. Inside me, my powers writhed in discomfort. They were clearly not fans of the portal system.

We kept going until we came to another branch, and another. Each time we carefully followed Veri's directions. I hoped like hell she could be trusted, and we wouldn't end up lost in the tunnels, or worse, come out in a Hel dimension.

Finally we arrived at the portal Veri had marked on the map. "Now or never," I whispered, stepping out into nothing.

Chapter 19

The wind blew my hair wildly about my face as I tumbled and tumbled down, down. And then things seemed to right themselves. I rolled out onto the hard ground of the high desert. I lay there panting, staring up at the sky until Kabita crashed into me with a grunt.

"It would have been nice if she'd warned us about the drop," Kabita panted.

"She probably did it on purpose," I said with a groan as I sat up. "I don't think she likes me."

Kabita snorted as she clambered to her feet. "More like she knows you don't like her."

I stood as well, stretching out muscles that were a little touchy, thanks to a solid landing. "Well, I didn't dislike her until she got all weird on me."

Kabita shook her head. "Whatever. Where are we?"

I didn't recognize anything, and yet I recognized everything. Lots of places in the High Desert look the same to an untrained eye, and mine was definitely untrained. I listened carefully and was pretty sure I could hear, very faintly, the sounds of battle.

"This way." I tromped off across the desert to the west.

"You sure?"

"Pretty sure."

Kabita snorted again. "How reassuring."

Ten minutes later the battle came into view. The dome was all but gone and the combatants were everywhere, spilling across the plain. SRA agents were desperately wielding their special weapons, trying fruitlessly to keep the war restricted to djinn lands. They were fighting a losing battle. Literally.

"What do we do?" Kabita asked. "Reactivating the wards isn't going to work. Too many of them are outside the area."

I thought it over. "Is there any way you can temporarily trap or confuse only one side?"

"You mean the djinn," Kabita said dryly.

"Yeah."

She stared at the battle. "Maybe. With a lot of help."

"Can I be of service?"

We turned to stare at the newcomer. Tommy leaned casually on his walking stick for all the world like it was a nice summer day, and he was out for a stroll.

"The barrier the djinn erected to keep humans off their lands," I said. "Can it be altered to keep djinn on the land, at least temporarily?"

He mulled that over. "Sure. Take some doing, though."

"But I imagine a shaman and a natural-born witch could manage."

He nodded. "I imagine."

"Good, because here's the plan…"

Trevor had pulled his men back behind the djinn curtain. I had no idea how the Sidhe had breached it, but they were tricky that way. The curtain had been designed as a barrier to keep everything out of djinn territory, and it had worked a treat for thousands of years in conjunction with giant Mongolian death worms. Until I came along and killed the worms. Yeah, not my brightest moment.

"All right, now!" I shouted.

Kabita and Tommy started doing their thing. I had no idea what exactly; I was too busy focusing on my task. I reached down to pull out my Earth power, but instead of letting it shimmer out through my skin as usual, I forced it into a tight channel through my amulet. The amulet stone glowed hot, bright blue, amplifying the Earth magic a thousandfold. Why hadn't I thought of this before?

Focus, Morgan.

I let it pour out of me in one continuous wave, building and building. And then I called them. I beckoned the Sidhe with all the power of Earth and ancient Atlantean magic. At first nothing happened. And then, one by one, the Sidhe turned and stared for a moment with surprise. Then they left whatever djinn they were fighting and walked straight toward the curtain.

As they passed through it, the djinn stormed after them. I knew they weren't going to stop. They were going to slaughter every one of the Sidhe they could get their hands on. And then the first djinn smacked face-first into the barrier. He paused, shook his head in confusion, and tried again with exactly zero success.

"Hurry it up, Morgan," Kabita snapped. "We can't hold this all day."

I poured more energy through the amulet. *Go*, I ordered them through the magic, *leave this place and go back to the Otherworld. You will not leave it again to fight the djinn.*

A greenish silver portal shimmered into existence in the middle of the High Desert. The Sidhe began to pass through two by two as the djinn continued to slam against the curtain, unable to leave their lands.

"What is the meaning of this?" Morgana suddenly appeared in front of me. Her face was twisted in an ugly snarl.

"You told me to end the war, Morgana. I'm ending it."

"This is not what I meant," she spat.

"Then you should have been more specific."

With an angry shriek, she stormed to the front of the line where Sidhe after Sidhe dove headlong into the portal. "Stop this at once. I command it!"

They ignored her, still caught in the thrall of my magic. She tried closing the portal, but it wasn't hers to command. She let out another angry shriek and stomped her feet like a petulant child.

"Morgan Bailey, you will suffer for this."

"Not if you want to accomplish whatever it is you and Alister Jones are planning. You need me, and you know it."

With a final blood curdling scream, she shoved aside the next warrior and stomped through the portal. The few remaining Sidhe warriors followed her, and the portal closed.

"Clear!" I shouted.

Tommy and Kabita let the curtain fall. Djinn warriors stormed out, bristling for a fight, but there was no one left. All the Sidhe were gone, and the SRA agents were back far enough they posed no threat.

"What is the meaning of this, Hunter?" The Marid bellowed, shoving his way through the crowd of warriors. "Have you chosen the side of the Sidhe?"

"I have chosen no sides, Marid. I have chosen to end a pointless war. There will be no more fighting."

"She started it."

I crossed my arms. "I finished it. At least for now. The High Priest did not send you here so you could destroy this planet with your ridiculous fighting."

I could have sworn he blushed, though it was hard to tell what with his red skin. "You assume much, little girl."

"And you need to learn to keep your shit together, big man."

We stared at each other for several heartbeats. "Fair enough," he finally said. "But if the Sidhe encroach on our lands again, there will be war, so you'd best be finding a way to keep them in the Otherworld."

"Working on it."

He nodded and beckoned his warriors to follow him. They all disappeared onto djinn lands. Just like that, the battle was over. For now.

"Holy…." Kabita shook her head. "Holy…."

"Shit?" I supplied.

"Yeah, that."

"That was quite the experience," Tommy agreed.

"Kalen, you can come out now," I said, barely raising my voice.

Kalen shimmered into visibility. I'd had no idea Sidhe could make themselves invisible. It was both cool and freaky, but Kalen had assured me it was a rare gift.

"It worked," he said with a grin.

"Thank goodness you can open portals as well as the queen."

He shrugged. "All royals can. Another nail in my coffin."

"Or jewel in your future crown. Your people will know the queen didn't open the portal, and they'll wonder who did. They'll know it was someone with royal blood."

"There is that." He glanced behind him to see Trevor approaching. "Better go. My lady." He sketched a bow and disappeared again.

"Explain." Trevor's words were sharp as he strode toward us. He was in full-on agent mode.

"Easy peasy," I said. "I had Kabita and Tommy hold off the djinn long enough so I could force the Sidhe out of djinn lands and through a portal back to the Otherworld. For now, the war is over, but it's probably a good idea to keep agents here, just in case."

He nodded. "I agree."

I drew him away from the others. "To change the subject, have you ever heard of our father purchasing a plot of land in Michigan?"

He stared at me like I'd sprouted wings. "Seriously? You're looking for, what, a vacation home now? Weren't you trying to save the world two minutes ago?"

I snorted. "Don't be an idiot. Inigo and I found a deed to

some land our father purchased before I was born. Do you know anything about it?"

"No." He sounded curious. "Is it important?"

"I think so. The land is in my name, too, but he died before I was born and my mother chose my name. How did he know?"

"How strange. Maybe Tommy knows?" He waved Tommy over.

I repeated my question for Tommy. "Nope," he said thoughtfully. "Your father never spoke of it."

My father never spoke of it. Interesting turn of phrase. "I didn't ask if my father had spoken of it, I asked if you knew about it."

Tommy's expression didn't change. The man was an enigma. "So you finally found the connection."

"The connection?"

"Well, if you're asking about Michigan, you must've found the connection. Your father never mentioned land there, but I once saw it in his memory. I knew it was important, I just didn't know how."

I stared at him. "You didn't think to mention this before?"

He shrugged. "Wasn't the right time."

Tommy and his mystical whatsis was enough to drive me crazy. "Fine. Anything else about it?"

"Just that one day you would need to go there."

"Well, I'm going there now that things are under control here. Apparently that's where Alister went."

He pondered that. "Interesting."

"I guess."

"Keep me posted in any case," Trevor said.

"I will."

He walked back to join his men, and I turned to Kabita. "Time to head back to Portland. It's time to go after Alister and finish this once and for all."

Chapter 20

I was surrounded on every side by swirling masses of dark, ominous clouds. Lightning streaked across my vision, nearly blinding me. My heart beat so loud, it was a wonder it didn't deafen me. Inside, my powers roiled, pushing at my insides like they wanted to destroy me in order to get free.

Why was this trip so much worse than the last? I pushed my powers down and moved on, ignoring my trepidation. Emory had assured me the portal system was safe. Once it was opened by a witch, anyone could pass through, including a Hunter with far too many powers for her own good. I'd managed it once, I could do it again.

In my mind's eye, I saw the path Alister had taken. Of course, I couldn't retrace his steps from Area 51, but Emory had assured me her portal would open into the first branch he'd taken. From there I retraced his steps as I remembered them from the ritual. At last I came to the final branch. Right or left?

Alister had taken right, so that's where I went. The portal shimmered in front of me, and beyond I saw the tall evergreens, grasses waving in the breeze, and farther on, a large body of water. It was the lake of the Amazons, the place of the last colony of Atlantis. This was definitely the right portal.

As I stepped out, wind swirled around me, lifting my hair from my cheeks. I smelled the trees, the fresh green of the grass, and the tangy scent of lake water. Behind me, the portal closed.

Oddly, I felt none of the disorientation or nausea I'd experienced traveling through the queen's portal. I wondered why? I'd have to ask Emory later. Maybe it had something to do with how the system worked, or the fact that it opened onto my own plane of existence rather than the Otherworld. It wasn't important at the moment.

I glanced around. As far as I could see, there wasn't a sign of civilization. No power lines, no houses, not even a picnic table. Had I gone back in time?

I heard an odd rumbling and looked up. Far overhead was the outline of an airplane. Still in my time. I admit I felt a little relief at that.

There wasn't a sign of Alister. I had no idea where to go, so I headed toward the lake. After all, it was where the Amazons had set up camp how many thousands of years ago. This was where they'd come, so clearly this place was important. This lake meant something.

Sand crunched under my feet as I stood at the edge of the lake. Water lapped at the tip of my boots. Still no sign of Alister, nor was there any sign a camp had ever been built here. It had been long ago, so that was no surprise.

I wandered slowly along the shore, scanning for anything that might show me where Alister was or what he was up to. Suddenly my amulet started burning. With a hiss, I yanked it from under my shirt. The stone glowed brilliant blue against the bright sun. Earth magic was nearby. Was it one of the Sidhe? Had they followed me?

Something a few feet out from shore caught my eye. A partially submerged stone, about the size of an apple crate, was glowing with a faint blue halo, identical to my amulet. Not Sidhe, then. Atlantean magic.

I kicked off my boots, peeled off my socks, and waded into the lake. Brushing moss and dirt from the stone, I could make out deep etchings within the rock beneath. They looked almost prehistoric. I frowned as I recognized the symbols. Ancient Atlantean. This was definitely the spot I'd dreamt about.

Recognition shivered through me as I realized that on this spot, millennia ago, my ancestors had created something, a colony they'd hoped would be a foothold in this new world. How and why they'd vanished I might never know, but they'd come here for a reason. The Amazons had followed for an even more important one. And Alister? He was here somewhere. I could feel it in my bones.

I waffled with what to do. On the one hand, I didn't want more years of washing by water to wear away the symbols on the stone. But to move it was like an archaeologist's nightmare. But what archaeologist in their right mind would ever believe the symbols were from an ancient alien race that had once visited our planet? A race whose DNA now lived inside of me, Jack, Trevor, and countless others. No, they'd lock me up. And then the SRA would find out the truth about Trevor and me. I couldn't have that.

Bracing myself, I tugged at the rock. It didn't budge. I boosted my Hunter strength with a touch of the Darkness. Still nothing. The rock must go deeper into the ground than I realized. I'd have to bring out some equipment later and move it properly. In the meantime, I needed a record of the stone and the markings.

I slipped my cell phone out of my pocket and snapped several photos. I made sure to get close-ups of the markings and wider shots of the stone with the surrounding area. My best guess was that this was some kind of marker for travelers in search of the colony.

Satisfied I had enough pictorial evidence, I waded back to shore, dried my feet on the grass, and pulled my socks and boots back on. I moved along the shoreline, searching for any sign of Alister. There were no footprints, broken grasses, or tree limbs to show me which way he'd gone. The man was the master escape artist.

As I walked around the curve of the lake several hundred yards from the portal, I stumbled upon what looked like an old campsite. Not Amazon old, but perhaps a couple of decades old. Someone had clearly been camping here for many years.

And it wasn't my father or anyone else who belonged on this land. My father had been dead longer than I'd been alive, and I hadn't even known about the place. I reached for the knife on my belt.

"And so at last, the prodigal daughter has arrived." Alister stepped out from behind a thicket of trees. The smirk on his face sent my blood boiling. "I wondered when you'd get here. Let the fun begin." He rubbed his hands together in glee.

"This isn't a game, Alister," I said. The knife's hilt was warm in my hands. I couldn't see the grimoire anywhere. Probably he'd hidden it somewhere nearby.

"Oh, but it is," he said, taking a step closer. "And I'm about to win it." His expression was one of happiness, but there was something in his eyes that wasn't quite right.

"Don't come any closer," I said, holding out my hand, palm facing him. I needed him not to be near me. I didn't know what I would do if he attacked. I didn't want to kill him, but I was a Hunter. I couldn't help myself. The Darkness inside me rose, spreading to my eyes. My vision started to tunnel down. I tried to push it back, but the Darkness would have none of it. It was in control, not me.

"Oh, there you are," Alister said, as if greeting an old friend. I swear to gods he giggled.

Images barraged my brain. Images of my father and Alister. Of my father fighting demons and vampires, and laughing while he did it. A shiver went down my spine. I recognized that laugh. It was the Darkness let loose to do what it loved best: kill. More images flooded my memories until one final one burned bright in my brain. Alister thrusting a knife into my father's chest.

I gasped, clasping a hand over my heart. I felt the pain as if it was my own. I half expected blood to seep through my fingers.

"Ah, so you can feel it. Very good." He seemed thrilled by the fact, his aristocratic features twisted in a parody of a smile.

There was definitely something off about him. More than usual.

"My father had this? These powers?"

"I don't know what powers you're talking about," Alister said tauntingly. "But your father did have something inside him he called the Darkness. It gave him more strength and power than anyone I'd ever seen. I wanted it. But even in death, he would not tell me the secret. Perhaps you will."

"If there is a secret," I said, "I can't tell you. I don't know what it is."

"Pity. I've been so hoping that you did. But that's all right. I can still accomplish all of my goals without it."

"And what are your goals?" Keep him talking. Keep him talking.

He smirked as he stalked toward me "That would be telling, wouldn't it? Let's just say I have a few party tricks planned."

"You mean you and the Queen of the Sidhe," I said.

His expression grew stiff. "I don't know what you're talking about." But it was clear he did.

I snorted. "Oh, please. You know as well as I do there's no way you could've opened the portal into Darroch's cell on your own. And since there isn't a witch alive who would help you, there's only one other person who could do it."

"Besides yourself, you mean."

How did he know that? "You've been working with the queen. She's the one who helped you kill Brent Darroch. Why?"

"Oh, just tying up loose ends, as it were. We didn't want anything getting in the way of our plans."

"So you admit you're planning something."

"Oh little girl, I'm always planning something." And with that he attacked. I was so distracted, I hadn't seen the gun in his hands until the bullet was tearing through my shoulder.

The scream that ripped from my throat was one of pure rage. I didn't even felt the pain. The Darkness rushed to the surface, pushing it out. I dropped the knife, and it stuck hilt up in the soft soil. Reaching inside myself, I pulled my powers out, running on anger and adrenaline. Icicles flew toward his chest before I'd even formed a thought. Unfortunately, while the ice was fast, it wasn't bullet fast. He dodged, and it splintered against the trunk of a tree. I threw another, this time managing to scrape the side of his cheek raw. A third whistled over his head as he ducked. I was out of ice.

I needed a new tactic. This time I went with fireballs, lobbing them one after another toward my target. He kept well out of the way, ducking and dodging behind trees and shrubbery. At least one of them gave him a good scorching as it passed by, though not enough to cause permanent damage. He started to run, but I sent out tendrils of Earth power, which wrapped around one of his ankles, yanking him to the ground. I strode toward him like a lioness stalking her prey. This was it. I was going to end this. Now.

Chapter 21

I walked toward Alister with a loose-limbed stride I usually associated with much more graceful people. I knew the Darkness shone in my eyes, or whatever the opposite of shining was. I felt it in me, writhing around, saturating every pore. It owned me. And in that moment, I didn't care.

Blood slid from the wound down my arm in a warm trickle. It dripped to the ground, and where it fell, tiny red flowers sprouted. Guess that's what I got for channeling Earth magic while bleeding all over the place.

Alister lay on the ground, pinned by my magic. I stepped closer, and one of his legs lashed out and caught me in the ankle. I went down like a sack of potatoes, pain lancing through my arm as the fall reopened the already healing bullet wound. So much for grace. I could feel that the Darkness was surprised. Maybe I wasn't as arrogant as the Darkness. Or maybe I understood human nature better. Magic or no magic, Alister wasn't going to lie down and give up. He'd fought his entire life pursuing an insane ideal of purity among the races. Or maybe, I should say, purity among humans by the destruction of anyone with magic. He wouldn't give up that easily.

I hit the ground with a jarring thud. It rattled me enough that I lost concentration. The tendrils of magic holding Alister to the ground dissipated, and next thing I knew he was on top me, pinning my legs. He punched me in the face. I turned my head and caught the blow on my cheekbone. It hurt like hell, and I'd have a nasty bruise, but at least he didn't break my nose.

I didn't have enough leverage to punch back, and besides, my right arm hurt like hell. So I clawed at his eyes with my left hand, hoping to blind him. My nails raked a bloody furrow down his forehead and cheek, and he howled in anger and pain. He raised his fist to punch again, but this time I caught it.

Channeling my Hunter strength boosted by the Darkness, I pushed his arm back, away from me.

Alister slid a long hunting knife from his boot and raised it above his head. It slashed out, bright against the sunny sky. I threw up my left arm to avoid getting my throat cut. A wide slice opened up on my arm, followed by white hot pain. Bright blood welled in the wound, slowly spilling out of the cut to slide down my arm. The Darkness was fascinated by the red. It wanted to stare at it. Taste it.

Gross. I pulled the Darkness back, and it did what it was supposed to: boost my strength, dull the pain.

I grabbed Alister's wrist and twisted it hard until the fine bones crunched beneath my fist. He howled again and dropped the knife. He hauled off to hit me again with his good hand, but I got there first with a karate chop to his Adam's apple. Gagging, he fell backward off me.

Kicking his knife out of the way, I grabbed mine off the ground and heaved myself to my knees. I moved over to straddle Alister. Pressing the blade against his throat, I leaned in close. A drop of blood slid from my arm onto his cheek, smearing with his own blood. He stared up at me with so much hatred and rage, it was a palpable thing.

"Where is the grimoire?" I demanded.

"Fuck you." In his cultured British accent, the words sounded odd.

"No, thanks. I like my men less evil. Now answer me. Where is the grimoire?"

He cackled madly. "You'll never find it."

"What do you want with it? What are your plans?"

"As if I'd tell you," he taunted.

He was right. He wasn't Darroch. Grandstanding was one thing, but no way was he going to spill his guts. Not to me. Not to a Hunter.

The Darkness roared back, angered that it couldn't control this one frail human. It raged inside of me, overwhelming everything I was.

"Fine," it growled with my voice, "then I have no need of you." I raised the blade with both hands and plunged it toward his chest.

A split second before the tip of the blade pierced his heart, someone grabbed my arm and wrenched it back so hard, it almost dislocated my shoulder. Pain screamed through my nerve endings, knocking the Darkness back a notch.

"No, Morgan, you can't do this."

I glanced up. Jack. Where the hell had he come from? I opened my mouth, but the Darkness was back. "Let. Me. Go."

"Morgan, listen to me. You must control it."

"He needs to die."

"Probably deserves it, yeah," Jack agreed. "But we need Alister. You can't kill him."

I threw back my head, and the Darkness howled, all the anger and rage spilling from me like a river of black through my soul. The part of me that was still half in control grabbed onto the Darkness and yanked on it, trying to get it back under lock and key. It fought me, but I wrestled it bit by bit back into my center, shoving it down and slamming the proverbial lid on it. With the Darkness where it belonged, I sagged, suddenly exhausted. Both arms hurt like hell, although they were already healing.

Jack rolled Alister over and yanked his hands behind his back. Pulling a set of handcuffs from the back of his jeans, Jack snapped them around Alister's wrists.

"What are you doing here?"

"Kabita sent me through the portal."

"Where did you get those?" I asked, still lying on the ground, too tired to move. The cool grass felt good against my cheek.

"Trevor," he said. He kept one knee pressed to Alister's back, but his attention was on me. "Are you all right?"

"Fine." I sat up, cradling my arm. Stung like a son of a bitch. "Could use a bandage."

"Stitches, more like, though it's healing okay." He pulled a handkerchief out of his pocket. "It's clean."

I wrapped it around the cut on my arm. The white cloth immediately turned crimson as blood soaked through the cotton. It would heal completely before I got anywhere close to a doctor. I winced as the wound in my right shoulder twinged.

"How did you convince Kabita to let you through?" I squinted up at him. The sun turned his hair to spun gold, but his ocean-colored eyes were hidden behind dark glasses.

"I'm your Guardian, remember? I have my ways."

"I didn't need you. Everything was under control."

He gave me a look. "Was it?"

I shrugged, wincing as the movement jarred my arm. "I wasn't in any danger."

"Physically, no."

I knew what he meant. If I'd killed Alister...

I shook my head. But I hadn't. Part of me was relieved. It freaked me out that any part of me wanted him dead.

"He won't tell me where the grimoire is or what he wants with it." I glared at Alister's inert form. He grinned back at me. For a guy in handcuffs, he was awfully chipper. Had he lost it? Because he was acting awfully weird even for Alister.

"Maybe you haven't found the right leverage," Jack said calmly.

I sighed. "What kind of leverage?"

"Is that your blood on his face?"

I glanced at the bloody mess drying on Alister's cheek. "Some of it. Some of it's his. I got him pretty good."

Alister made a sound of derision. I wasn't fooled. I'd seen his pain. Felt it deep inside me. The Darkness had enjoyed it.

"The blood of a Hunter on an open wound. Interesting, don't you think?"

I shrugged. "Not really. Happens all the time."

"With vampires, yes. Sidhe, maybe. Demons. But never humans."

I blinked. "What are you talking about?"

"You're not just any Hunter, are you, Morgan?" Where Jack was going with this, I had no idea, but I decided to play along.

"Uh, sure. I guess not. Atlantean DNA and all that."

"But more than that."

I frowned. "I don't follow you."

"You're a Hunter who once died."

Things started snapping into place. "Yes. I was killed by a vampire."

"A vampire who drained your blood."

"Yes." I glanced from Alister, who was looking decidedly green, to Jack, who looked decidedly smug. "That's why I died." Well, that and the severe injuries and blood loss.

"But they revived you. Brought you back to life or so they said."

I frowned. "Yes. That's what they said."

"They were wrong."

"What?" I was confused. Alister looked like he wanted to puke.

"Remember what happens to a human with Atlantean DNA when exposed to the vampire virus?"

"They, uh, change into a Sunwalker. I'm not a Sunwalker."

"That remains to be seen. But do you know what else happens?"

"I'm guessing you're about to tell me."

He smiled. It was slow and deadly and absolutely chilling. "The virus remains in your system, waiting. Waiting for a new host. For someone else to infect. Someone who doesn't have Atlantean DNA. A pure human with no defenses." He stared down at Alister, his gaze ice cold. "And as Jones here is fond of bragging, he's pure human. Except for the witch blood, of course, but that doesn't count."

"Oh my holy shit," I whispered. "Are you telling me I infected Alister? He's going to be a vampire?" Kabita was not going to like this.

Jack yanked Alister to his feet. Alister whimpered a little. He wasn't looking good. "That's what I'm saying...unless..."

Alister's eyes lit up with hope. "Unless what?"

What was Jack doing? There was no cure for vampirism. Alister had to know that.

"Give us the grimoire, and I'll give you the cure."

It was all I could do to bite my tongue. Alister snorted.

"There's no cure," he scoffed, but I could still see the hope in his eyes. And the madness.

"The humans have no cure," Jack said softly. "But as you well know, I am no longer human. I'm over nine hundred years old, and I am by no means the oldest of us. Do you honestly think we haven't found a cure by now?"

Was he serious? Surely he couldn't be, but he seemed to be telling the truth. Then again, Jack had ways of skirting the truth, using it to suit his needs. I supposed in a way, it was his job. Anything to protect the Key of Atlantis. Which, in this case, happened to be me. How had I gotten so lucky?

"Then why haven't you used it to stop this scourge?" Alister demanded. Good point., He was at least sane enough to think somewhat logically about this.

"Because it only works after a person has been infected and before they turn. Those we've cured never knew what happened to them. Those we couldn't save...we deal with in other ways. We prefer not to allow human governments to get their hands on such things. It's better this way."

I could see the thought process in Alister's mind. Hope warring with cynicism. Hope won out, or perhaps he thought he could get us to lower our guard, turn the tables on us.

"Very well," he said finally. "Give me the cure, and I will take you to the book."

"The grimoire first, then the cure. Do you think I don't know what you're planning?"

"I die, and I take its location to the grave."

Jack snorted. "You die, and I stake you. Then I go get a witch to find the damn book."

Alister swallowed. "Fine. I'll take you to it. But only if you swear on your oath as a Templar that you will cure me of this disease."

Jack stared at him for a long time. "On my oath as a Knight Templar, I will cure you."

Alister nodded once, then led us away from the lake. As we passed into the dim light beneath the trees, I shivered. What the hell was going on?

Chapter 22

Alister led us into the woods, wandering from tree to tree in what seemed like an aimless manner. Every now and then, he'd stop and stare into space until Jack nudged him in the back. After about fifteen minutes, I stopped.

"This is bullshit," I snapped. "You're just jerking our chains. Show us the grimoire, Alister."

"I'm trying." He blinked in confusion. "It has to be around here somewhere," he muttered. "I left it here. Here. I know here. I said here."

Okay, hello funny farm. "Um, Alister. Focus. Where's the grimoire?"

"Here. There. Everywhere." He giggled.

Jack and I exchanged glances. "You think he's faking?" Jack asked, voice low.

"Not sure. He's been a little off since I found him." Or he'd found me. Whatever. "Come on, Alister. The grimoire. Focus."

"She promised, you know. That's why I did it."

I eyed him, but he was gazing at the leaves above his head in rapture. "Okay, I'll bite. Did what?" I asked.

He stared at me blankly. "What?"

Jack snorted. "Bet he's faking."

"Wouldn't be too sure, but he's useless right now."

"So, how are we going to find that book?"

I grinned as a thought sparked. "Atlantean magic."

He frowned. "The amulet?"

"Why not?" It had helped me find things before. I pulled it from beneath my shirt and held it up. At first nothing happened. But as I turned in a slow circle, the amulet warmed and the stone began to glow. I kept turning, and the heat and light faded.

I walked slowly in the direction I'd been facing when the

amulet lit up. The glow of the stone intensified, as did the heat, until the amulet nearly burned my hand. In front of me was a large tree with one of those holes where a knot or something used to be. Alister giggled.

"This must be it," I said. Reaching carefully into the hole, I felt around until I touched something solid. It felt like a plastic bag. I grabbed it and pulled out the grimoire sealed inside one of those gallon freezer bags. I handed it to Jack. "Not the most original of hiding places."

"But it would have taken forever to find it if you hadn't had the amulet."

He had a point.

Book in hand, Jack dragged Alister to the portal, me tagging along behind like a good little Hunter. Alister struggled against Jack's hold.

"You promised," he spat, nearly foaming at the mouth. "You said you would give me the cure. On your oath."

"And I will. When the time is right. But first you are coming with us. I'm not done with you yet." He shoved Alister into the portal, stepping in behind him.

I stared at the portal for a moment, feeling a little weirded out. Things were escalating so fast, I didn't quite know what to think. Shaking my head, I entered the portal.

We were halfway through the system toward what I assumed was Portland when things went wrong. Alister suddenly stumbled, nearly ripping his arm out of Jack's hold. Jack lost his balance and fell back into me, throwing me into the wall of the tunnel.

I wish I could describe properly how it felt. It was like having a live electrical wire stabbed through your chest. Not a tiny one like from an electrical outlet, but one of those big ones from the power lines. Every nerve in my body was on fire. My muscles spasmed out of control. The last thing I saw as I slumped to the floor unconscious was Jack's face.

# # #

She stood before the lake, straight and tall, dressed in the flowing blue robes of a priestess of the Temple of the Moon. She was partially translucent like a ghost. Or a memory. I stepped toward her, unsure what to do or say.

"Hello, Morgan."

My eyes widened. She knew me? I mean, I was me for once? Not someone else?

"Hello. How do you know my name?"

She turned then, and I recognized her. "Amaza."

A smile curved her lips. She gave a little bow. "Last of the Atlantean priestesses. First of the Amazons. To meet you is a great honor."

"Believe me, the honor is mine." A freaking Amazon. How cool was that?

She nodded. "We all have our parts to play. Each essential in its own way."

"What are you doing here? I mean, this is a dream, right? Why am I dreaming about you?"

She stepped closer. "I brought you here."

"That wasn't an accident, me falling into the portal wall?"

"We needed to speak. This was the only way."

I frowned. "Speak about what?"

"It is nearly time."

"What do you mean?"

"You must find the Four. It is nearly time."

"The Four? I don't understand. What Four?"

"Earth. Air. Fire. Water. You must find the Four."

"I'm sorry, I don't..."

"The Spellwalker is needed."

"Emory? What's she got to do with this?"

"The Soulshifter must reveal herself."

"What the hell is a Soulshifter? Please, tell me what you're talking about."

She pressed a finger to the middle of my forehead. "Wake up."

#

I awoke, blinking against the flash of white hot lightning. Jack was kneeling over me, shouting at me.

"Would you shut it?" I snapped. "My head hurts bad enough without you yelling."

"Are you all right?" he asked.

I rubbed my chest. "A little sore, but I think I'm okay. You?"

"Fine. I'm not the one who connected with the portal energy."

"Yeah, wouldn't recommend it." I staggered to my feet and saw Alister lying unconscious on the floor not far away. "Did you knock him out?"

Jack shrugged. "No more than he deserved. Let's get out of here."

I wanted nothing more. Jack leaned down, grabbed the still unconscious Alister by the wrist, and began dragging him along the tunnel.

"There's no cure, is there?" I whispered. Jack didn't answer.

We stepped out of the portal into Emory's backyard. Above us the sky was dark, the stars dancing their never-ending minuet. A small fire burned cheerfully in one of those metal fire pits. All four witches stood inside the circle: Emory, Kabita, Veronique, and Lene. Each still held their white candle. Cordelia was there, too, clearly enjoying her moment of magic.

The only difference was that outside the circle stood Eddie, Inigo, Haakon, Trevor, and Tommy. I blinked. Why was the whole gang here?

The witches stopped chanting and blew out their candles.

Behind us, the portal snapped shut. Jack and I waited with Alister lolling between us while Emory banished the circle. Then she waved us to gather around the fire pit.

"How did it go?" Kabita asked, not even glancing at her father.

"We got the grimoire," I said, holding it up. The firelight glinted against the wrought gold and gemstones. "Of course, we still don't know what it means and Alister hasn't told us his plans yet."

"He will," Jack said grimly.

A warm hand wrapped around mine, and I turned to find Inigo standing close behind me. He said nothing, but the look in his eyes warmed me inside and out. I squeezed his hand, acknowledging our bond, and he squeezed back.

I love you.

It whispered through my mind like the remnants of a dream. So I whispered it back. I knew he heard me because his blue eyes began to turn gold. The dragon was close to the surface, as it often was when our emotions ran high. It was a relief to see it. It meant Inigo was himself again. Maybe not the same as before, but himself.

"Trevor, why are you here? And Tommy? What about the djinn?"

"I left my men to guard the border," Trevor said grimly. "All is quiet for now."

"That's a relief." I rubbed the bridge of my nose, suddenly feeling exhausted. "No sign of the queen?"

"None," Trevor said. "But knowing her, it's only a matter of time. I'm here because I'm hoping whatever is in that damn book has something to do with what's going on, and I plan to help you stop it."

It was a safe bet. I had no doubt Alister was in this war nonsense up to his eyeballs. Whatever his plans were, they somehow played into the queen's.

Jack tossed Alister into a chair. The man stirred a little and groaned. He was coming around. Good. We needed answers.

I knelt in front of him and waited, my mind still full of my dream of Amaza. What did it all mean? I knew Emory was involved, but the rest of it was a mystery, one maybe Alister could solve.

He opened his eyes and stared at me. "He promised."

"And he'll fulfill his promise once you tell us what you were going to do with the grimoire."

"Say the spell, of course." He smirked, some of his cockiness back.

"It's in a form of ancient Atlantean no one alive knows."

His smile grew wider. "The queen herself promised to translate."

How did the queen know ancient Atlantean? And an obscure dialect at that? "Why? What does it do, this spell? What's her angle?"

He cocked his head to the side and stared at me for a long beat. "Truly? Don't you know?" He grinned a little madly. Okay, a lot madly. "It will finally rid the Earth of this pestilence with me as supreme leader of all!" He cackled. Yep. Definitely gone around the bend. Several bends, probably.

"That doesn't make any sense," I pointed out. "The queen would never allow anyone but herself to reign."

He snorted. "All I know is that our goals align, and she has promised her assistance."

"If you believe that, you are a bigger fool than I imagined. The queen has but one agenda. Her own."

"And the friend of my enemy may be my enemy, but she is a means to an end."

"Your end, no doubt."

"Perhaps," he said calmly, "but you'll be long gone. And

that's really all that matters."

"What do you mean?"

He smirked at me in that smug, superior way of his. Rat bastard.

"What my father means is his goal of eradicating every non-human on the planet will have been achieved. Every magic practitioner destroyed. Nothing else matters to him."

I stared down at him. "The queen would never agree to that. Not unless her people survived."

"Oh, there's definitely more to this," Kabita agreed. "Much more. That's Alister's plan, such as it is. I'm not even sure he knows what he's doing anymore. In any case, I'm certain the queen's plan is very different, but only she knows what it is."

"Tell us what you know, Jones," Jack said, leaning right into his face. "If you want the cure, you'd best spill everything."

"Cure?" Kabita asked softly.

I swallowed. "Jack thinks I might have infected him."

She stared at me for a long moment, then nodded. "I suggest you cooperate, *Dad*. I hate to have to explain to the boys that you turned vamp, and I had to stake you."

Yeah. Couldn't see that going down well with Kabita's brothers. Even if they were MI8 and Hunters in their own right.

Alister stared from his daughter to Jack and back again. "All I know is she required certain people to complete the task. The Key, of course." He nodded to me. "She tried to create a new Key with Darroch's help but failed miserably."

He was talking about Jade. The queen and Darroch manipulated the Dragon Hunter to their own ends, those ends being a replacement for me. Not that Alister was innocent. I was pretty sure he'd had the same plan, but they'd gotten to Jade first and ruined things for him.

"But there were others," Alister continued.

"What others?"

"I don't know specifically, but she said they were required to finish the spell."

"A spell you don't know how to perform." And one he thought would make him king of the world.

He shrugged slightly. "I *will* change the world."

My guess was the queen was lying out her ass. The spell would achieve one goal: the queen's. But the book was written by an Atlantean, which meant it wasn't a Sidhe spell or even a Witch spell. It was Atlantean and therefore met their goals, not the queen's or Alister's. My guess was she planned to pervert it to her own ends somehow. I needed to know who these "others" were.

"The Four," I gasped.

"What are you talking about?" Kabita asked.

I pulled them away from Alister so he couldn't hear. "In the tunnel, when I got knocked out, I had a dream. A vision."

"You were knocked out?" Inigo demanded.

I waved him away. "I'm fine now." My chest still hurt, but I wasn't going to point that out. I didn't need anyone fussing. "I had a vision of a priestess of Atlantis. She told me it was almost time. She told me I needed a Spellwalker." Haakon's eyes flitted to Emory. "I also needed a Soulshifter, whatever that is."

Kabita stared at me. "A Soulshifter. Is that what she said? Did she say why?"

I shook my head. "She didn't. And she didn't answer when I asked her what one was. Anyway, she also said I needed to find the Four: Earth, Air, Water, and Fire. I have no idea what that means. The four powers, maybe?"

"You already have those," Trevor pointed out.

"And more besides," Inigo said drily. "She must be referring to something else."

"If I may," Eddie said, stepping forward and taking the grimoire from me. "I believe the answers are here." He flipped open the book. Scattered among the lines of the spell were symbols. Some I recognized, others I didn't. "This," he said, tapping his forefinger on a page, "is the Atlantean symbol for water."

I nodded. I recognized it from my amulet.

"And this." He moved his finger to the symbol next to it. "This is for the ancient water Titan, Nereus."

I stared at him. "You mean...?"

"This is the symbol for me. I am one of the Four."

Chapter 23

"Are you kidding me?"

Eddie peered at me over the rims of his glasses. "I'm afraid not, my dear. There are, ah, a few things you don't know about me."

I snorted. "That's an understatement if ever I heard one. Care to share?"

He smiled, his round cheeks and fringe of white hair making him look more like a cherub than a powerful Titan. "Not just yet."

Inigo took the book from Eddie. "Who are the other three?" He peered at the page where Eddie's symbol lay, then flipped to another page. "Wait. This symbol under the symbol for fire. This is my brother's symbol."

I peeked around his broad shoulder, ignoring his chocolatey s'mores scent. "What do you mean? What's Drago got to do with this?"

"Well, technically, it's the symbol for the Dragon King, but that happens to be Drago at the moment."

"That makes sense," Jack said from where he stood next to the fire pit, one booted foot braced against its rim. "My guess is the other two symbols are for the rulers of the djinn and Sidhe. Air and Earth."

Eddie nodded. "That would be my guess as well."

Earth, Air, Fire, and Water, just as Amaza had said.

"Oh, wonderful. The two people who are trying to kill each other are the two people we need for"—I waved at the book— "whatever this spell is."

"Unfortunately, yes." Eddie flipped through a few more pages, studying each one carefully. "Honestly, I haven't the foggiest notion what this spell involves or what the results will be, but it's clear these four people are critical to its success.

161

Along with a Spellwalker and a Soulshifter to create the spell together. And you, Morgan. The Key to it all."

"Freaking fantastic."

"My sentiments exactly." Eddie snapped the book closed, his expression about as serious as Eddie ever got. "Whatever this spell is, it was important enough for the Queen of the Sidhe and Alister Jones to work together. My guess is that power of some kind is involved. It always is with these people." He sniffed as if he smelled something bad. I always felt that way around Alister.

"Alister," I said, striding toward him. He stared up at me from where he lay curled on the ground. "You ready to tell us the truth? Or do you want me to let you turn? Trust me, it's not fun." I'd never seen anyone turn vampire, but I doubted it was in anyone's Top Ten Fun Things to Do.

He glared at me as if looks could kill. Gone was the sophisticated British MI8 agent. The rumpled man on the ground looked half feral. He refused to say a word. Instead he rocked back and forth, his eyes slightly unfocused. He was getting worse. Dammit.

"We can't just go around casting random spells," Emory said, speaking up for the first time. She and her coven stood nearby. It was her backyard, after all. "You can't just blunder in blindly. Spells require intent, and without knowing the intent to put into the spell, things could go very wrong. Do you have any idea the kind of hell you could unleash on this planet?"

I shook my head. "The Atlanteans would never have done such a thing." Of that I was sure. The dreams convinced me. "This was something they meant for good. Something significant. They were a people of peace before...before the virus destroyed them. Whatever this spell is, it's important."

"My father and his little Sidhe partner probably figured they could pervert it to their own ends. That's what he does." Kabita scowled at Alister. "It's no doubt why they tried to make Jade into the Key so she could replace you." Kabita stared at her father, her face a mask. I had no idea what she was thinking. I didn't imagine it could be good.

"Peace," Eddie blurted.

We all turned to stare at him. "What?" I asked.

He had the book open again. He pointed to a page. "This symbol is Atlantean for peace. I recognize it. I think it was meant to bring peace to the world. Somehow."

"Well, that explains it." I crossed my arms. "As far as Alister is concerned, peace is eliminating anyone not human."

"And the queen returning to Earth as supreme ruler of all the races," Inigo murmured.

"Using each other to their own ends. Who do you think would win?" I asked.

He snorted. "My money's on the queen. Alister may be devious—or he was before something sent him over the edge—but that woman is pure evil."

"Not pure evil," I said. "Just nuts with a side of rampant egocentricity."

"We need to perform the spell, Morgan," Eddie said, his tone urgent. "We must ensure the spell occurs as the ancients planned. That it is not twisted by evil desires. This" —he placed his palm flat on the book— "is what we've all been working toward. This is what you were meant to do."

Eddie was leaning a little far into cosmic destiny for my liking, but he wasn't wrong. This was the reason the amulet had chosen me. So I could finish this. It would have been nice if it had asked me first.

"If we're going to do this, how are we going to get the rest of the Four to agree to it?" I asked.

"Drago's not a problem," Inigo pointed out. "You're family, remember. Dragon kin."

"Oh, right. The whole Fire Bringer thing." Apparently I was

the answer to some ancient dragon prophecy. I still had no idea what it meant, but it was important to the dragons in a big way.

"I'm a little more worried about the Marid and the queen. The Marid would probably be okay with it except he's kind of irked with me right now. And the queen is batshit."

Kabita's eyes narrowed. "Unless she believes it's in her best interests to cooperate."

I grinned. "Excellent. We've got to make her believe if she helps us, she's somehow going to get what she wants."

"A Sidhe kingdom here on Earth. Masters of us all," Jack said drily. "Surely she'd never believe we'd allow that."

"She's lost what's left of her mind," I pointed out. "Just like Alister. We can get Kalen to help us. Maybe he can think of a way to trick her. He's crafty like that." After all, the man had hid in plain sight for hundreds of years.

Jack nodded. "That works."

"One problem," Eddie interrupted. "If you'll recall, the Marid can't leave djinn lands."

"Why is this a problem?" I asked.

Alister started laughing, a grating cackle that belonged in a cheesy movie with a cardboard villain. "Surely you're not that stupid."

I whirled on him. "Watch it, buster. What do you mean?"

He howled, nearly doubled over from it like I had said the funniest thing ever. "Oh, this is rich. You really don't know, do you? You think I was in Michigan for my health?" Tears were streaming down his face.

"I'm glad you find this so funny," I snapped.

And then it all fell into place. The grimoire. The deed to my father's land. Alister's obsession with Michigan. My dreams of the Amazons, the last colony of Atlantis, and the lake.

"We have to do this spell in Michigan, don't we?"

Alister just laughed.

# # #

"Hunter, I would like to help you, but I am currently in the middle of a war." The Marid was pacing back and forth in his underground office. If he wasn't careful, he was going to wear a hole in his fancy Persian rug.

"Not at the moment you aren't," I reminded him. "The Queen of the Sidhe is back in the Otherworld, and SRA agents are patrolling the borders. For now, everything's quiet."

"But for how long?" He shook his head. His skin gleamed red under the large candelabra hanging from the roof of the cave. He let out a deep sigh which expanded his massive chest. "Even so, I cannot leave djinn lands. I am bound or have you forgotten?"

I hadn't. I'd seen it all happen in my dreams, or visions, or whatever they were. "I get it. The last High Priest of Atlantis tricked you and bound you to this land where you've been stuck for ten thousand years. But I remember something else." I eyed him carefully. "He told you it was necessary. That one day you would perform the task he had set for you, and you would be free."

He snorted. "Well, then, bring the party on down here, and let's get to it."

I shook my head. "It has to be done in Michigan where the last colony stood." I still had no idea why, but I knew beyond a shadow of a doubt that was important. "There is no other option."

"Then you are out of luck."

"I don't think so."

He stared at me for a long moment. "Explain."

"The priest had to have known what was going to happen.

He had to have planned this with the Priestess of the Moon Temple. That's why he sent his son—Sunwalker Sentinel by the way—there with the half-blood princess. The last living member of the royal bloodline."

"I am listening."

"When humans attacked the Temple, trying to destroy the Atlanteans and the virus that was turning them into ravening vampire-like creatures, the priestess, Amaza, already had an escape plan in place. A very elaborate one at that. In fact, she started the entire Amazon nation to protect the princess and the last of Atlantean knowledge. She even brought the princess to the New World and the spot of the last Atlantean colony. She could not have done that on her own. She had to have had help putting the plans in place before it all went down."

"What does that have to do with me?"

"She must have made those plans with the priest. They worked on this together." I had no proof, of course. It had never been part of my dreams, but I was sure of it. "He would have known you would need to be in the New World to perform whatever task he had set for you. He wouldn't have put you too close, though, or it would have given the location away to his enemies. He bound you to the land both to keep you safe and make sure you didn't go near the place until it was time."

"I still do not—"

"But he would have known you'd have to be released eventually so you could do what he wanted you to do. Pay back your debt to him."

He crossed massive arms over an even more massive chest. "Is that so?"

"Yes." I nodded, sure of myself now. "He would have given you a key."

The Marid snorted. "He gave me no key."

"Yes, he did," I said with a grin. "Me."

With the Marid agreeing to help us, there was only Morgana left. And she was going to be tricky.

"This is insane," Inigo said. He stood next to me in Emory's back room, a portal shimmering in front of us. I could smell the faint scent of green from the Otherworld.

"This is the only way to get to the queen. I have to talk to her. There isn't another way."

"Shit," he snarled. "I'm going with you."

"No, you're not." I laid a hand on his arm, giving it a squeeze. "I will not put you in danger."

"Oh, but you'll stick your head in the lion's mouth."

"The Sidhe can't hurt me." At least I hoped they couldn't. I was betting my Earth power combined with Kalen's help would keep me from getting my head chopped off. Or something else equally uncomfortable.

The portal pulsed. "It's now or never," Emory said from where she stood at the edge of the circle. "I can't hold it open much longer."

I nodded. I pressed a kiss to Inigo's lips, then stepped through and into the Otherworld. The portal snapped into place behind me. I was truly on my own.

Channeling a light touch of Earth power, I let it shimmer along my skin. The light green sparkle barely stood out against the weak, greenish sun and the lusher greens of the forest. Here and there I made out dead trees, dried up vines, and moldering grasses. I could only imagine what the queen would do to my world if she got her paws on it. We had enough problems of our own without her mucking with things.

I began walking slowly through the forest. It was like moving through a dark hallway. Only the tiniest bit of light found its way through the canopy of leaves, leaves that were starting to turn brown. Something that should never happen in the Otherworld where spring was perpetual. Morgana's poison was spreading.

I ducked as a sentient vine made a half-hearted lunge for my head. When it missed, it dangled there, limp and dejected. I made out dark spots along its surface. Some kind of plant disease.

I continued, picking my way around fallen dead trees, patches of scrubby undergrowth, and the occasional carnivorous flower that still struggled to survive in the dying forest. There was no avoiding the scrape of thorns from the brambles that were encroaching on the queen's land.

I pressed on, finally exiting the jungle. The plain leading to the castle, once lush with grasses, was now barren, the ground dry and cracked as if it there hadn't been rain in a hundred years. The faint wind stirred up little dust devils here and there. It was a thousand times worse than my last visit. The castle was a crumbled ruin in the distance. Gods, this was bad.

"Well, who have we here?"

I whirled to find Morgana standing behind me. The Queen's Guard ranged out behind her. I didn't recognize the new captain, who she'd clearly appointed after discovering Kalen's true identity. If she'd have been smart, she'd have kept him close. Easier to kill him that way.

I winced. That was the Darkness talking, or so I told myself.

"Hello, Morgana. Nice to see you." Liar, liar, pants on fire.

"Don't be coy, Hunter," she sneered. "It doesn't suit you."

"Really? I thought it fit rather well." She looked astonishingly bad, a grotesque parody of her former haunting beauty. Her hair had gone from a beautiful golden red to dull dishwater blond. Her eyes were even muddier than before, sort of swamp water meets mud pie. Even the whites had gone a sort of yellowish-brown. Her skin looked like old paper, thin and cracked. Her dress hung from her thin frame like a gunny sack.

Twin spots of rage blossomed on her pale cheeks. "Come to join me at last?"

"I'd rather die."

"That can be arranged."

"I'm sure it can. After all, your alliance has done wonders for Alister Jones."

She waved a hand airily. "That weakling. So wrapped up in his own agenda he could not see his nose in front of his face. So easily manipulated." She giggled.

"You put a spell on him, didn't you? That's what's messing with his mind."

Her grin was pure evil and half crazy. "I was surprised he agreed to it, but it was necessary. He is tied to me now. Until death."

Wonderful. The queen had put her mojo on Alister, and he'd gone crazy town when she had. "I have a proposal for you. Something you might find of interest."

I could tell she wanted to ignore me, have her guards chop off my head, but curiosity got the better of her. She couldn't help herself. "Oh, really?"

"Yep. See, your buddy Alister and I have decided to team up."

She stared at me for a moment. Then she blinked slowly. "Team up?"

"Mmhmm. See, he's got this interesting little book with a spell in it. He says we can all get what we want if we just agree to cooperate and do the spell."

A sly look crossed her face, and she crossed her arms. Her fingernails were ragged and dirty. "Really."

"Well, between you and me, Alister is crazy pants, but I'm

thinking you and I can get what we want, at least."

"I doubt that."

"Think about it, Morgana. You want the Sidhe to attain their rightful place, correct? Equality with humans in our world. Not stuck off here in fairy land."

Her eyes narrowed and her lips thinned. "Is that so?"

"I have no problem with that, Morgana. I believe in equality and all that. I just want peace."

She snorted. "You're a Hunter. Peace is not in your nature."

"True," I nodded, caressing the hilt of my knife to remind everyone who they were dealing with. "But I would give almost anything to destroy the vampires and keep the people I love safe. This spell can do that, but I need your help."

"Anything?"

"Yes. Anything. That's what a Hunter does. Or haven't you figured that out yet?"

Her smirk grew wider. "Very well. Let us talk about how we can help each other."

"Stop the war. Swear to peace with the Marid. No more threats. No more attacks. Then we'll talk."

She sniffed. "Why should I do that?"

"Because once this is done, the war will be over. Permanently. Isn't that what you want?"

Her smile chilled me to the bone. "Done."

Chapter 24

The lake lapped against the shore in its eternal bid to take over the land. Maybe one day it would but not today.

At the edge of the lake stood all the factions necessary for the spell. Morgana and her guard were at one side, looking like they'd like to slit everyone's throats. I'd tried to convince her to come alone, but it had been futile.

The minute she'd arrived, Alister had gone into a frenzy. He'd cried and begged, screaming "You promised!" over and over. Morgana had sneered and turned her back, leaving Alister sobbing on the ground.

Opposite the Sidhe contingent was the Marid with his own guard. He seemed redder than usual, probably because he looked like he wanted to rip Morgana from stem to stern. I'd been right about him leaving djinn lands with me. Holding my hand, he'd been able to pass through whatever invisible barrier had stopped him before.

In the middle, my friends huddled together, including Eddie and Drago. Alister, still in handcuffs but with added leg irons, sat on a rock not far away. He wasn't looking good. Emory was there, her skin unusually pale. She tried to hide her shaking hands in the folds of her broomstick skirt. She'd probably never worked with a spell like this before, and she definitely hadn't been caught between two races who wanted to tear each other apart.

The only person missing was Kabita. She'd promised to deliver a Soulshifter, and until she arrived with one, we were at loose ends. How long could I keep things from exploding?

A faint crackling, sizzling sound heralded the appearance of the portal and another traveler. Jack had said it was the same sound the aurora borealis made. Having never seen, let alone heard, the aurora borealis, I'd have to take his word for it.

Kabita stepped from the portal, two people hot on her heels. I recognized one of them, although it took a moment. He'd changed drastically.

"Mikey?" I called, stepping toward him.

He grinned. "It's Mick now. New name for a new life."

I grabbed him by the shoulders and scanned him up and down. Last I'd seen him, he'd been a seventeen-year-old junkie living a mere slice above homelessness. He looked healthy, happy, filled out.

"My gods, you look amazing."

"Been clean almost a year now, thanks to you." He wrapped me in a hug, squeezing hard. "Thank you," he whispered.

I fought back tears. It wasn't like I'd done anything major. But seeing him like this, so different, made me unbelievably happy. "I'm glad."

"He's not the Soulshifter," I said, turning to Kabita.

"Nope. She is." Kabita nodded at the girl standing beside Mick. She was a little shorter than me, a little thinner, with hair that had obviously been bleached blonde from a much darker color and eyes that were too big for her face. She looked about the same age as Mick.

"Morgan, I'd like you to meet my girlfriend, Abbie." Mick wrapped his arm around the girl's shoulders and gave her a squeeze. Abbie beamed at me.

"Hi," she said, sticking out her hand and giving mine a shake. "Nice to meet you again."

I blinked. I'd never seen this girl before in my life. "Again?"

"We've met before, but of course you don't remember. I looked a bit different then."

"Sorry, I don't..." I stared at Kabita helplessly, but she just shrugged.

The girl's smile widened even more, if that were possible, and she let out a laugh. "You wouldn't know me as Abbie."

"Then what would I know you as?"

"Call me Zip."

#

Those of us who knew Zip — myself, Jack, Inigo, the Marid and his people— stared at her. She laughed merrily as if this were the biggest joke in the universe.

I cleared my throat. "Zip is dead. I watched her soul leave her body."

"Uh-huh." She pointed at her chest. "Soulshifter."

The Marid stepped forward, derailing my train of thought. Not that it needed help. "Soulshifters are extremely rare," he rumbled.

"And they're what, exactly?" I asked.

He tilted his head and stared at Zip as if he could somehow pull her apart molecule by molecule and see the truth within. "Our physical bodies are nearly impossible to kill, as you know, but since our natural state is energy, our 'souls' as you call them, remain conscious after the body dies. It is possible, though rare, for the soul of a djinni to become stuck in the body of a mortal being. And when that body dies, it shifts to the next, and the next."

"Mortal. You mean a human."

"Among other species, yes. It can only happen if the host's previous soul has already fled but before any kind of, er, deterioration has set in." He meant decomp. Ew.

"You're telling me Zip's soul is stuck in that girl's body?" I peered at her as if I could see Zip's Marilyn Monroe figure somewhere in the slight girl.

Abbie giggled. "Don't feel bad. Imagine how long it took me to come to grips with it all, and I knew what I was."

"You're really Zip?" I asked.

"In the flesh." She winked and giggled again, a light, tripping sound. Yep. That was Zip all right.

With a cry I wrapped my arms around her, squeezing her tight. Tears welled in my eyes and trickled down my face. "I thought you were dead."

"The rumors of my demise have been greatly exaggerated, I assure you. But it's nice to see you, too. Would you please let go? I do believe you're strangling me."

I gave a watery chuckle and let go. "I still can't believe you're alive. And you found Mikey? I mean Mick."

"Long story." She shrugged. "I'll tell you sometime. But Kabita says you need my help."

I nodded, managing to force my scattered mind to focus. "We have a spell that requires a Soulshifter."

"Well, I have to admit, I'm not really that great at being a Soulshifter yet. Still trying to figure stuff out. Do you know what I have to do?"

"Ah, no. We haven't translated the spell yet." Only the queen could do that, and I sure as hell didn't trust her.

"Can I see it?" Zip asked.

"You read obscure Ancient Atlantean dialects?" Kabita asked with a lifted brow.

Zip laughed. "Not exactly, but I've come across some weird shit lately. Oh, hi, Emory." She waved. Emory waved back. So, they knew each other. My worlds were colliding in a very odd way.

Kabita handed Zip the grimoire, and she studied the pages with a furrowed brow. "Oh, this isn't an Atlantean dialect," she finally said.

We all stared at her. "It's not?" I asked.

"Nope. It's djinn. Very old djinn." She handed it to the Marid.

"It is, indeed, an old dialect of our language." His voice was a low rumble. "I can understand the mistake. The djinn did not have their own written language, so they borrowed one from their neighbors, the Atlanteans. We came from the same planet, after all."

"You can read it?" I asked.

"Of course."

I shot a glare at the queen, who was looking decidedly pissed off. "It's not something a Sidhe could read?"

"Definitely not. This language died with our planet. I am one of the few djinni left who can read it."

Which made absolute sense. The High Priest had deliberately written the spell in a language so ancient only the Marid could read it. Clever boy.

"Can you tell what the spell does?"

The Marid opened his mouth but before he could answer, there was a shout from Trevor. "Morgan, quick!"

I hurried over to where Trevor was guarding the chained Alister. Something was wrong. Kabita's father was doubled over, and his skin was doing some weird thing like it had worms in it or something.

"What the hell?"

Trevor shook his head. "I think he's changing."

Alister's back bowed, and I caught sight of his face. His lips were pulled back in an ugly grimace, his canines suddenly longer than they should be. His eyes had gone strangely cloudy. No doubt about it. He was definitely morphing into a vampire.

"Shit. The sun is still up. If he changes here, he's going to die."

"Let him." I hadn't realized Kabita had joined us.

I gave her a startled look. "Are you sure?"

Her face was blank. I couldn't read her feelings at all. "Dead sure. Let him dust."

"Kabita," Alister moaned. "Please..."

"Please, what? Forgive you for all the damage you've done? For the evil you've created in this world? I don't think so. You're about to become a vampire. A *vampire*. One of the things you hate most. One of the creatures we hunt. It's time to end this once and for all."

Guilt ate at my insides. I had done this to him. I had turned another person, a human, into one of the monsters. By accident, of course. I'd no idea my blood still carried the virus, that I could create a vamp. I felt sick.

"Don't you dare feel guilty," Kabita whirled on me as if she could read my mind. "He made his bed. He can freaking well dust in it." And with that she stormed away.

"You promised a cure," Alister moaned.

"There is no cure," I told him softly. "There never has been."

He whimpered. "I don't want to die."

I felt almost sorry for him then. He was so far gone, he probably hadn't had a true plan in months. He'd just been going through the motions as his brain slowly deteriorated. He was a shell of the man he'd once been.

Helpless, Trevor and I watched as Alister Jones began the inevitable change from human to vampire. I saw the moment it happened, the moment the creature in front of me was no longer Kabita's father or my nemesis, but became the mortal enemy of human kind. And then his skin caught fire, and he burst into so much ash and dust.

I would like to say I didn't cry. Alister Jones didn't deserve my tears.

But I did.

Chapter 25

I returned to the group with Trevor. They studiously avoided looking at me, except for Inigo, who wrapped an arm around my shoulders and kissed my forehead. The warmth of his love wrapped around my heart, and I sent the emotion back, knowing he'd feel it too.

"I think I know this spell," Zip squealed, clearly unfazed by watching someone like Alister go up in smoke. "Kabita, remember when you helped us stick that demon from my school into one of those bubble things between worlds?"

"Excuse me?" I said. "Demon at your school? What?"

Zip shook her head. "A long story. We'll do coffee. I tried calling you for help, but you were in Paris."

Chasing after Alister Jones. My heart gave a painful lurch. "Right."

"So Kabita helped out. She stuck the demon into this bubble thing."

"Interdimensional pocket," Kabita muttered.

"Right," Zip chirped. "This is like the reverse spell, but badass."

"So, we're pulling something out of an interdimensional pocket," I said.

"Not just anything." Zip grinned. "Something major. Something old. Like super old. Whatever is in there has been there for, like, thousands of years."

Okay. That was terribly unspecific. "No clue as to what? Or who?"

"No," said the Marid as he leaned over Zip's shoulder. "But the priest wanted whatever it is out. So out it is."

Mick was giving the Marid sidelong looks. Couldn't say I blamed him. The Marid was getting awfully chummy with Zip, and I knew for a fact she'd been in love with him once upon a time. Unfortunately, having a guy's claws rip through your chest, even by accident, tended to put a damper on amorous feelings. Besides, Zip was human now. Mostly. Her new heart beat for one man: Mick. I couldn't be happier for them. For the Marid it was too little, too late.

"All right, then I guess we do this. Who and what do we need?"

"I need to perform the spell along with Emory," Zip said. "The initial spell is fairly simple. Shouldn't take long. When we release whomever is inside the bubble, we start part two."

"There are two parts to this damn thing?"

"Yep. Second part is where the others come in. It's… a little more complicated."

"For now," Emory spoke up, "everyone clear the area and let us set up."

It was a quick matter of Emory closing the circle and calling the four corners. Then Zip did an invocation in what I could only assume was the djinn language. It sounded odd to my ears, sort of sing-song with lots of rolling *R*'s. My brain couldn't compute it as a language. Then the two joined hands and began chanting.

The space between them grew opaque. I saw a human-shaped figure as if far off in the distance, clouded with fog. It drew closer and closer. Then, with a loud *pop*, someone appeared in our dimension, kneeling between Emory and Zip. The two of them backed up, giving the newcomer room.

Slowly the person stood up. It was clearly a woman, her side to me, long hair covering her face. She was dressed in odd clothing: a tight band of leather binding her breasts and snug leather breeches covering her legs. Was she an Amazon? How could an Amazon help us?

The figure turned to face me and tilted her head back. Dark auburn hair fell away from her face, and I froze.

"Hello, Morgan." Her voice was as I remembered it, as was every line of her face.

It was the princess from my dreams. The last of the royal bloodline of Atlantis.

#

I chugged down an entire bottle of water almost without taking a breath. Then I sucked air into my lungs. I was feeling marginally less dizzy. I'd had to get away from the rest of the group for a bit before I had a meltdown.

"Easy." Inigo rubbed my back. "Don't overdo it, or I'll be peeling you off the ground."

I leaned against the tree trunk and closed my eyes. Gods, I felt like I was going crazy.

"Are you all right? What happened?"

"It's not every day your dreams come alive," I said, wiping a hand across my forehead.

"Remember my dreams about the last Atlantean princess? The half-blood that escaped the massacres at the palace and the Temple of the Moon?"

"That's her? How is that even possible?"

I told him about my dreams of Michigan and the Amazons. "I think they brought her here to keep her safe. When they realized this outpost had been destroyed, too, and the vampires and Hunters were already here, they stuck the princess in that interdimensional thingy to keep her safe. That was probably Plan B or whatever."

"So she was stuck there, unageing, for thousands of years?"

"Exactly."

"Then how did she know your name?"

"No freaking clue." I was definitely going to have to ask her about that.

"Morgan, can we talk?"

We turned to find the princess approaching. Her accent was musical and like nothing I'd ever heard before, but not heavy. She spoke English quite well. Gods, it was weird as hell seeing her outside my dreams.

I nodded to Inigo. He handed me another bottle of water and then strode back to join the others.

"All right," I said. "Talk. Let's start with how you know my name."

"The amulet."

I touched my necklace. "This old thing?"

"While it was in your possession, it sent me information. Images, knowledge, experiences so I would know what the world had become."

I wasn't sure how to feel about the amulet as an eavesdropping advice. "Princess— sorry, do you have a name? I can't just keep calling you 'Princess' all the time."

She seemed to ponder that. "Sharai."

"That's not your name." I don't know how I knew that, but I did.

She lifted one bronzed shoulder. "My true name would be impossible for you to pronounce. Sharai is close enough. Besides, I... like it." She said it as if liking something were a foreign concept.

"All right, Sharai, what the hell is going on?"

She smiled. "Amaza said you would be powerful. I just didn't realize how powerful."

I narrowed my eyes. "Amaza told you about me?"

"Of course. You are her descendent, after all. She knew every one of her bloodline from the day her first daughter was born until the end of time."

I blinked. That was a bit much to grasp, so I focused on one clue. "I'm a descendent of the Moon Priestess?"

She inclined her head. As her hair caught the sunlight, I realized it wasn't the auburn I'd assumed, but more of a dark plum color. I doubted it was Lady Clairol. She was half alien, after all.

"Um, I think I need to sit down." I let myself slide to the ground. "Okay, start at the beginning."

"You are not the Key, Morgan."

"Excuse me?" All this time, everyone had been going on about me being the Key. And now the princess—Sharai—was telling me the opposite?

She shrugged. "Not the true Key, anyway. More like a temporary one. You've been holding the power of the true Key until they could return."

"Let me guess. You're the true Key."

"Yes."

"And all these crazy super powers belong to you."

She nodded. "They were never meant to stay in the amulet as long as they did. The amulet was meant to be delivered to me, but it got waylaid. The powers needed a human host, and so they found Jack, and through him, you. Part of the spell is to return those powers to me."

I felt both relieved and oddly sad. I'd gotten used to my powers. They came in handy on a Hunt. "I don't know you."

"But you do. You've dreamed of me, as I have dreamed of you. You have done your task well, but a human was never meant to hold power like this forever."

"According to those in the know, I'm not truly human."

She smiled. "Not entirely, no. But mostly."

I thought about it. Everything was clicking together. I nodded. "Okay."

"It's true, you know."

"What is?"

She stared at me for a long time. Finally she said, "Sunwalker

Sentinels could pull energy from the sun and use it to boost their power during battle. When they turned, they took that ability with them, becoming Sunwalkers."

"I am not a Sunwalker." My tone was less than convincing.

"No," she agreed. "You are something else. That is the thing that is true."

I don't know if I stopped breathing or passed out or what. The next thing I knew, my head was swimming and my vision had fogged over.

He stood before me, heavy robes gently swirling in a wind I couldn't feel. In every other dream I'd been him. I'd never before seen his face, but I immediately knew who he was.

"The last High Priest of Atlantis," I whispered.

"One and the same. But you may call me Re." A broad smile made his perfectly straight nose crinkle and deepened the laugh lines around his eyes. In the weird half-light I couldn't tell if his eyes were brown or black.

"You're kidding, right?" Re was an ancient Egyptian solar god, not an Atlantean Priest.

"Hardly." His smile widened. "Where do you think most ancient human religions came from? Humans have always found it easier to equate technology and power with magic and gods."

True that. Even I, who knew better, found it easier to call what I did "magic."

I glanced around me at the desolate landscape. Not a scrap of vegetation anywhere. Barren rock formations cast long shadows even in the dim light.

"What is this place?"

"It is a rest stop of sorts. Between the worlds."

"Why am I here?"

"It's time."

My heart rate hit the stratosphere. I have no idea why, but I was afraid.

"Time for what?"

"Why do you think the Heart of Atlantis chose you?"

I hated when people answered a question with a question. Re could give Tommy a run for his money, but I decided to play along. "Because I'm strong. I'm a Hunter."

That seemed to amuse him. "There is no human alive, Hunter or not, strong enough to channel all the powers of the amulet."

"I do." Granted, it'd been rough, but I was figuring it out. More or less.

"Ah, but you are not entirely human."

I shrugged. "So I've got some Atlantean DNA. Just means I was able to access the amulet in the first place. No biggie."

"Ah, but it's a very big biggie." Re stepped into my personal space. "Yes, the amulet needed an Atlantean to activate it, but it needed all the races to download."

I blinked. "Excuse me?"

He touched my cheek with the tips of his fingers. Whisper-soft, as if I might run. "You, my dear Morgan, carry the blood of all the races of this world. And of mine."

I swallowed hard, trying not to freak out. What on earth did he mean? "I'm human." Maybe if I repeated it often enough, I'd believe it.

His smile was patient. "You are human. From one of the first families the Atlantean people met when we landed on your strange, new world. They did us many great favors, your family, and spent much time in the royal palace. The women of the clan were great beauties. Is it any wonder one of our royals fell for your ancestor?"

"The princess. The one you saved. The one I dreamed about. She was my ancestor, too? Not just Amaza?" I'd suspected it, but I wanted confirmation.

"Yes. Among others."

I stiffened my spine. I had to know the truth. "She is why I could access the amulet. And the other races?"

Re took a step back as if realizing his nearness made me uncomfortable. "Have you ever wondered why your mother named you Morgan?"

"I know why. She named me for my father."

He smiled. "Alexander Morgan had nothing to do with your naming except indirectly. He did, after all, get his name from the same place you did."

"What do you mean?"

"I was young and reckless once," a new voice broke in.

I whirled toward the newcomer. "Morgana."

She grinned, suddenly looking like her old self. Her sane self. Her plump red lips parted to reveal the tiny gap between her front teeth. Her almost sheer white gown draped perfectly around her slight curves. Apparently it knew better than to flutter in the breeze. That, or where she was, there was no breeze.

She waved her fingers at me. "A youthful indiscretion. What can I say?" She shrugged. "Your ancestor was delicious."

"Remember, Morgan," Re said, "the Sidhe and humans once lived together on your planet. Intermingling was common."

"Lots of people have Sidhe blood," I said. Not that most of them knew it.

"But how many carry the blood of the Fairy Queen?" He waved his hand, and before my eyes the scenery shimmered, changing from desolate landscape to a hospital room.

I recognized the woman in the bed. It was my mother. Younger, thinner, and full of both sadness and joy, hugging a baby to her chest. Me.

I swallowed hard, watching as my mother rocked me back and forth, whispering reassurances in my newborn ear. A tiny fist escaped the blanket, and she laid a kiss on my knuckles. "What shall I name you? Maybe after your father. He would have liked that. Alexis? Alexandra?"

Beside the bed I saw a shifting of light, sparkles twirling in the air forming a human shape. The shape bent down as if to murmur something in my mother's ear. A smile spread across her face.

"I know," she said to my baby self. "I'll name you Morgan."

As the image shimmered away, I stared at the Queen of the Sidhe. "It was you. You made my mother name me after you."

She smiled shyly. "As your entire line has been named after me since the day I gave birth to your many times great-grandfather."

"This land. Did you have anything to do with my name being on the deed to this land?" I demanded.

She smiled at me, and I knew it was so.

"Earth power." I swung back to Re. "She's the reason I can channel earth power."

He nodded.

"The rest?"

He gave the queen a look which had her stamping her feet in irritation. But she disappeared only to be replaced by the Marid.

"What the..."

He smiled at me. "Hello, Morgan."

"Um, hey. How are you...how are we...?"

"Related?" He seemed amused by my discomfort.

"Yeah."

"It's a rare thing for a djinni to spend time with a human, but your many times great-grandmother was something else. Strong. Intelligent. Shaman of her people. She was one of the first humans I met when we came to the New World. And I was hers from the day we met until the day she died."

I swallowed. "How many children did you have?"

"Three. But only one was mostly human and stayed with her mother. The other two were mostly djinn and came to live with me."

Something snapped into place. "Zipporah. She was your daughter...my aunt." I was pretty sure there were a whole bunch of greats attached to that, but whatever. I realized I'd been wrong. Zip and the Marid had never been in love with each other; they'd loved each other the way family does. "Why didn't you tell me?"

"Because, little one," he said, brushing his knuckles gently along my cheek, "if you had known, you would not have been able to do what you needed to do."

I wouldn't have been able to attack him or release him from Albrecht's

185

spell. I wouldn't have been able to allow Zip to die. I closed my eyes against the sudden tide of sadness.

"You're the reason I can channel Air."

He nodded, his smile filled with pride. "The best I've ever seen a human wield it. You are truly my granddaughter."

The lump in my throat grew impossibly larger as he'd wrapped me in a hug. It was like being hugged by the Hulk. Only, you know, a red one.

As I wrapped my arms as far around him as they'd go, he disappeared. "Bring him back."

Re waved his hand. "There will be time for that later. For now, you need to know a few more things about your heritage."

Another figure shimmered into view. I stared, mouth open. "Drago?"

"Hey, kid." He crossed massive arms over his black biker jacket, looking as badass as ever.

"Oh, gods, don't tell me we're related. That's so gross."

He grinned at that. "We are, but don't worry. It's on my mother's side so you're not related to Inigo. Much," he added with a wink.

I groaned. I guessed even if Inigo and I were related, there were a couple hundred generations between us. Still, that had such a major ick factor.

"How are we related exactly?"

"Something like a thousand years ago one of my dragon ancestors got jiggy with one of your human ancestors. Had a kid." He shrugged his massive, black leather clad shoulders as it were a normal, everyday occurance.

"Thanks. That's very specific," I said drily.

"Point is, we're very distant cousins and because of that, you can channel Fire."

"And you didn't think to mention this earlier?"

Drago stabbed a finger in Re's direction. "He told me not to. Said you weren't ready yet. I guess you are now, and you know what I know. See you at the party." And with that he flashed out. No shimmer for big, bad dragon boy.

Holy frakk. I was part dragon. I didn't think my mind could take anymore.

My brain was whirling in so many directions I needed to sit down. Scratch that. I needed to lie down.

Before I could so much as find a comfy rock, another person shimmered into view. "Eddie?"

He beamed at me. "I have waited a long time for this moment, Morgan Bailey."

"But...but..." I sputtered to a stop, reigned in my quickly scrambling brain cells, and tried again. "We're related?"

"Unfortunately not." He seemed truly saddened by the fact. "Your ancestral line died out over one hundred years ago. Or rather, the part of the line that lived underwater did. There are still a few of you roaming about above the surface." He led me over to a cluster of rocks perfectly shaped for sitting. "You are the first of your line born in a century with the ability to channel Water. That was why I was sent. To mentor you and help you when the time came."

I sat and stared at him at a complete loss for words.

"Don't worry," he said, giving my hand a squeeze. "You are mostly human. You just have extra sprinkles." His eyes twinkled, and I laughed.

"Oh, Eddie, what am I going to do?"

"What you were born to do, my dear." He leaned forward and gave me a fatherly kiss on the cheek. "Now I must go prepare. I will see you soon. And don't worry. I've got someone to help keep the queen in check." And with that he was gone.

I sat there staring into the distance, mind racing. It was too much to take in. Finally something broke through the crazy.

"Sharai was right. I wasn't meant to keep this power forever, was I?" I asked, turning to Re.

He watched me intently, waiting.

"I was simply meant to hold it," I continued. "It's why I am the Key."

Still his impossibly dark eyes watched me.

"And every key was created to open a lock."

I knew what I had to do.

Chapter 26

"Are you well, Morgan?"

I blinked, staring at Sharai for a long heartbeat. "Yes, fine." How long had I been out of it? The dream had felt so real, but everyone was going about things like nothing unusual had happened.

She jumped to her feet. "Come. There is much to do." She whirled and strode toward the rest of the group, her long hair swinging purposefully.

I stared at her retreating back. I now knew for sure I wasn't a Sunwalker. Jack was wrong. And I was sort of relieved, but sad, too. The whole living almost forever thing wasn't something I was ready to face even though I knew Inigo would outlive me by a few hundred years at least. I didn't even want to think about that. But my abilities...

I shook my head. We had bigger demons to fry. I hauled myself to my feet and went to join the others.

Sharai was in full princess mode, ordering everyone about. They were setting up a circle reminiscent of those Emory and Kabita had created, but much bigger and more involved. When she finally had everyone arranged to her satisfaction, she waved me over to stand in the middle of the circle facing her.

By now the sun had long set and the moon had slid high in the sky. The princess's face was cast in shadow.

"The amulet," she said.

Frowning, I pulled the amulet from under my shirt. The blue stone in the center glowed softly in the moonlight.

Sharai held out the grimoire. "Place the amulet in the setting."

I carefully pressed the amulet into its place amidst the gold filigree. For a moment nothing happened, and then, as before, a beam of brilliant blue light shot from the stone to the heavens.

It was as if it were lighting the way...somewhere. I started to remove my hands from the book, but the princess trapped them there with her own. We stood there, the book between us, hands touching as the stone grew increasingly brighter.

The princess began to murmur in ancient Atlantean, her eyes fixed on the shining stone of the amulet. I didn't know the words, so I focused on the sound of her voice. Around us the others began to chant. It was the same three words over and over. Again in Atlantean. I really needed to get Eddie or somebody to teach me that damn language.

Beneath my fingers, the gold filigree grew increasingly warm. Hot, even. It felt like it was burning my skin. I tried to pull away, but Sharai was surprisingly strong. She held my hands in place. I couldn't help wiggling at the discomfort. Forget discomfort—downright pain.

It felt as if the heat was burning a hole through my flesh. I whimpered and something rose within me. Flames danced along my skin, but I hadn't drawn them. The Fire was reacting not to me but to the princess. What the hell?

Before I could open my mouth, the queen broke the circle. She ran toward us, expression intent, eyes focused on the amulet. I knew what she wanted. She wanted the amulet, the power, for herself. That had been her plan all along.

Sharai gasped as if in physical pain. Her eyes widened. The flames swirled around me in a whirlwind of Fire. The tips of my hair danced and sparked. I felt nothing but comforting warmth except in my hand which still hurt like hell.

As the queen laid one hand on the book, tugging it slightly, the flame danced from me to her. It touched her hand, singing her fingers immediately. She howled in pain and jerked back. Too late. The flames ripped up her arm and across her chest. Before I could open my mouth, she was a pillar of flame burning brightly against the night sky. I stared at her in horror as the screaming went on and on, and the air filled with the stench of roasted flesh. My stomach heaved, and it was only sheer willpower that kept me from puking up my guts.

And then the flame blinked out, and all that was left was a dark, smoking spot on the ground. No bones. No ash. No nothing.

"Is she dead?" I whispered.

"Yes." Sharai looked strained. "But we must continue or the amulet will destroy us all."

"How can we without the queen?"

"We need another Sidhe. One with power."

"Me." The voice had come from outside the circle. Kalen stood there, not in his warrior garb but in a simple pair of jeans and a T-shirt. Weird. "I will help."

"Hurry," the princess whispered.

Kalen took the queen's place, and we returned to chanting. The Fire still danced along my skin as if waiting for something. And then it happened. As if ripped from my body by a giant hand, the flame left me entirely and hovered in the space between us before smashing into the princess's chest. She winced but otherwise seemed unmoved.

"What the —"

"Focus," she gritted out.

I nodded and tried to concentrate on her words, but it was difficult. Sound was muddy and dim, like I was underwater. My vision grew wavery, but it looked like my skin was covered in beads of sweat. Not sweat. Water.

And then the Water turned to Ice, and I began to shiver. Mist rose from the ground at my feet, creeping up my legs, banishing any iota of warmth left by the Fire.

As before, it felt as though a great hand grabbed hold of the power in me and yanked it out by force. I gasped and rocked back on my heels at the sheer strength of it, and then watched as a ball of water and mist wrapped around a core of ice slammed against Sharai and sank into her chest. It looked painful.

Two down. Three to go. I wasn't an idiot. My powers were leaving me one by one and entering her. Which, I told myself, was as it should be. But with the loss of each one, the empty space inside me grew.

The Earth left me slowly, its tendrils retracting little by little until there was nothing left. And finally the Air. It didn't hang around, but vanished in a final whoosh that kicked up a tiny whirlwind around my feet. The hollowness in my soul threatened to eat me alive. Tears ran down my face at the loss. Sorrow overwhelmed me. I felt as if I'd lost part of myself. Sharai at last opened her eyes, and I saw my powers, hers now, dancing within them. Earth, Air, Fire, and Water. She had them all.

With a final, lyrical line, she ended the spell and banished the circle. Although dismissed, the others remained, staring at us. The princess and I still held the book between us, the amulet stone now gone dark. I let go of the book and sank slowly to my knees. Lost.

Chapter 27

I don't know how long I sat there on the cold ground with the princess standing guard over me. She wouldn't let any of them touch me, not even Inigo.

I didn't cry other than those few tears. But I wanted to. I felt...numb. Everything that had made me *me* for the past year or so was gone. I was a Hunter again. Almost normal. No more superpowers.

Something stirred inside me, and I gasped, placing my hand over my chest. There was something still in there.

"You see," Sharai said softly, offering me her hand. "They're not all gone."

I took her hand and rose to my feet. "I don't understand. The Darkness. It's still there."

"Of course it is. It was yours all along. As it was your father's before you."

I stared into those violet eyes, questions racing through my mind. "You're going to have to explain."

She smiled and removed the amulet from the grimoire. She lifted the chain over her head so the amulet hung in plain sight. Then she tucked the grimoire into what amounted to a ten thousand year old fanny pack.

"Walk with me."

We strolled along the banks of the lake, moonlight shining down on us. The Darkness stirred inside me, comfortable with its newfound space. It drank in the energy of the night, sending power to every molecule in my body. The Darkness was definitely still there and stronger than ever. And yet I felt oddly more control than before, energized, excited.

"Tell me."

"There was once a village here," she said, turning to gaze out over the water. "The last outpost of the city of Atlantis. The vampires came and along with them, the virus. And the Hunters. We could not save it."

"I know," I said. "I figured as much."

She sighed. "I told you of the Sunwalkers."

I nodded.

"There was rumor that at one time in our ancient past, there were those among the Atlanteans who could channel energy not from the sun, but from the very darkness around us. The shadows. The night itself. It all gave them strength. But it was not rumor. It was truth. You carry this power within you, a power passed down your line from generation to generation. Asleep until need arose. The rest of the powers you held for me, but the Darkness has always been yours. In fact, it was partially this ability of yours that also allowed you to hold the rest of the powers. It's why the amulet chose you."

"Why do I have this ability?"

She smiled gently. "They were so in love, you know. Anyone could see it."

"Who?"

"Amaza and my warrior. They called him a half-breed, and some looked down on him, but he was a powerful one. Destined for greatness. If not for the virus."

"You mean the son of the last High Priest of Atlantis." I remembered him, too, from my dreams. He'd died with his father in the cave where Jack found the amulet.

She nodded. "She was pregnant the night I came to the Temple. It was a great secret, of course. A child of a Sunwalker Sentinel and a Moon Priestess. Shocking breach of protocol. And the child's powers were enormous. You, Morgan Bailey, are a descendent of that power. That is why you are what you are. "

"I was told I'm more than that."

Her smile widened. "Indeed. At one point or another, your ancestors got very friendly with beings from all the races.

Another reason you could hold my powers for me."

"Why didn't you keep them? Why put them in the amulet?"

"I was a child. I lacked control. The priest and Amaza were afraid I'd be found. I needed to pass as human. And so I did for a very long time. But eventually, time ran out."

"Now what? What will you do with all this power?"

"Realign the races to bring them back into balance. Bring peace to this world as I was always meant to. It won't happen overnight, of course. In fact, it could take many generations. But it will happen." She seemed absolutely convinced of it.

"Where will you go?" I figured she needed some kind of headquarters somewhere.

"With your permission, I will stay here. On this land. What is left of my people still lies beneath these waves. I will need it if I am to complete my mission."

I shook my head. "I'm not sure about all of this. I just stopped two crazy people from destroying everybody. What keeps you from doing the same?"

"This world cannot exist without all of us, Morgan. We all play a part. We all need each other whether we know it or not. The planet is unbalanced. If this does not change, it will die and all of us along with it. We need to change things together, but you know as well as I that humanity isn't ready to face reality. Change is slow. I will have to do a lot of work behind the scenes."

I trusted her because Amaza trusted her. So did the High Priest and all the others I'd dreamt about over the years. And, if all I'd learned was true, her blood flowed in my veins.

I nodded. "You can stay here as long as I'm alive to own this land." Since I owned half of it, thanks to my father, I could promise that much, at least.

She chuckled. "That will be a very long time indeed."

"What do you mean?"

"Look inside, Hunter. Beyond the Darkness. What lies there?"

Frowning, I searched with my inner eye. Sure enough, hiding beneath the Darkness glittered something else. It was light and kind of sparkly but elusive. As if it wanted to hide. "I can't make it out. What the hell? Did you put that there with the spell?"

"Oh, no," she said reaching out to squeeze my shoulder. "That, too, was there all along. It was hidden beneath all the rest."

"What is it?"

"You, my friend, have been Kissed by Eternity."

The vamp swung at me with his right fist. I dodged out of the way and jabbed his diaphragm. I heard a rib crack, and the Darkness grinned. I kept it on a tight rein, using its strength but not allowing it to get out of hand. It was easier now with the other powers gone.

The vampire snarled, baring fangs. "Die, Hunter," he hissed, charging again.

"Seriously? Is that all you've got?" I gave him a good hard kick, which only made him madder. He staggered to his feet and came at me again, nearly connecting this time.

I told myself not to be a jerk. I needed to end this and move on. I might have been Kissed by Eternity, but I had to be more careful now than ever.

Sliding the machete from its sheath across my back, I waited for the perfect moment. One strike and the vamp's head tumbled from its body. A split second later, it exploded into dust and ash.

With a satisfied smiled, I wiped my blade off in the grass and slid it back into its sheath. It felt good to be out hunting ordinary vampires again. Things were back to normal, or as normal as they ever got around here.

Glancing around Waterfront Park to make sure no one had seen me, I strode back to where I'd parked my car. I climbed into my Mustang, revved the engine, and headed home just as the sun began to turn the sky gray.

Jack had stayed behind in Michigan with the princess to help her start her mission. I admit I was baffled by his choice. I'd gotten used to him being around.

"But you're my Guardian," I'd said.

His smile had been a little sad. "No, Morgan. I'm the Guardian of the Key. And you are no longer the Key." He nodded to the princess. "She is."

"So you leave. Just like that." Typical Jack.

"Afraid so."

Part of me had been sad to see him go, but most of me was relieved. He really didn't have a place in my life anymore. It was too full of more important things.

Kalen, Morgana's nephew, returned to the Otherworld with the promise that the Sidhe would leave humanity alone. He was hellbent on restoring health and vitality to the Otherworld. If anyone could do it, he could. I only hoped he'd stay true to his word and keep his people out of my world.

With Darroch, Alister, and Morgana dead, there was no one left to pull Jade's strings. Using an experimental drug, the SRA was able to wipe her mind of the last few years and give her new memories. Good ones, I hoped. In any case, they sent her back to the UK. I only hoped she'd stay out of trouble. I so did not want to have to track down a Dragon Hunter. Talk about messy.

The Marid returned to his land, free at last from the chains that had bound him for so many millennia. Still, he seemed happy enough to remain with his people. Where was he going to go? Their planet had been gone longer than most of them had been alive. Tommy promised to keep an eye on them just in case.

Zip and Mick returned to Portland along with most of the rest of us. They promised to stay in touch, and I had no doubt I'd be seeing them around. Eddie, too. He said he enjoyed running his shop too much to pack up and leave. Portland was his home. He liked it weird.

Veri had invited me to visit her lingerie shop, next door to Emory's. "Don't take this the wrong way," she'd whispered. "But you could use a new bra." She wasn't wrong about that. Mine was digging into my armpit. Besides, it would give me an excuse to scope her out, find out what she was hiding.

Emory returned to her cute little shop and her run-down Victorian. She promised to have Inigo and me over for dinner. Emory and Cordelia struck up a friendship, although Cordy swore Bastet liked me best. Emory also asked Kabita to join her coven, but Kabita politely refused. She was a solitary witch.

In fact, she decided to take a few weeks off to spend with her family in London. Alister's death hit them all hard. He may have been a bad guy, but he was still their dad.

In the meantime, Haakon had agreed to stay on at the PI firm and help me and Inigo with cases. The women of Portland may never recover.

As for me and Inigo, well...

I stood staring at myself in the mirror. It had been two weeks since the big hoopla in Michigan. I'd gotten an email from Sharai—how bizarre was that?—letting me know things were going well. She and Jack were settling in and drawing up plans for whatever came next. She promised to keep me in the loop. I wasn't holding my breath; I had other shit to do. Vampires were still a problem. Demons, too. I didn't have time to worry too much about what she was up to and the long-term ramifications of what we'd done. At least we'd stopped the bad guys, and that was all that mattered.

Before he left Michigan, I'd told Drago I was sorry I was no longer a Fire Bringer. "What do you mean?" he'd asked.

"I'm no longer Kissed by Fire. It's gone. I can't be a Fire Bringer anymore."

A slow smiled spread across his face. "Wouldn't be so sure of that."

I'd had no idea what he meant, but a few weeks later, he sent me the oddest gift. Inside was a note that read: For the next generation of Fire Bringers. The box held a dragon's claw. I had no idea what to make of it until later…

I squinted at my reflection. Had I changed? Could anyone see the difference? I sure couldn't.

"Morgan, immortality isn't visible." Inigo entered the bedroom with a stack of laundry. We'd moved in together after we got back. It seemed right and neither one of us wanted to spend any more time apart. We'd already wasted too much of it.

"I'm not immortal," I insisted. "I'm just going to live a really, really, really long time."

"Which is all right with me," he said, setting the laundry on the bed and coming up behind me to give me a squeeze. "I plan on keeping you around just as long."

I grinned. Dragons mated for life. And they lived a really, really, really long time, too, which I guessed made us the perfect match.

"Well, I wasn't looking for my immortality," I said.

"What were you looking for?"

"To see if it showed."

He frowned. "If what showed?"

"The baby."

His reflection stared at mine in complete puzzlement. "What b—" His eyes widened. "Are you—?"

I nodded. "Surprise. We're having our very own dragon

baby."

He let out a shout that probably gave the neighbors heart attacks. Then he whirled me around and laid a kiss on me that could have gotten us arrested if we were in public. I guessed he was happy.

I had no idea what lay ahead for us. Being a parent scared the crap out of me. And what did that mean for Hunting? So many questions whirled in my head. So many fears and worries. But I knew we'd come through them all.

Together.

The End.

A Note From the Author

Thank you for reading Kissed by Eternity. If you enjoyed this book, I'd appreciate it if you'd help others find it so they can enjoy it too.

Want to know what Zip and Mick have been up to? If you're curious to know where our favorite djinn and the boy Morgan saved have been since the end of Book 3, be sure to check out their further adventures in Sunwalker Saga: Soulshifter Trilogy: Fearless, Haunted, and Soulshifter.

Want to know what happens next? While I tried to bring everything full circle and tie up loose ends, there are probably still a few unanswered questions. Like, "What's up with the hot Viking, Haakon?" and "Who are the mysterious witches who helped save the day?" Never fear! Look for a brand new series starting this spring. It's set in the Sunwalker world and many of your favorite characters will be making appearances. Particularly one very sexy Viking Sunwalker.

Spellwalker (Sunwalker Saga: Witchblood – Book 1) will be coming your way spring of 2015.

Be sure to sign up for my mailing list so you don't miss out!

http://sheamacleod.com/mailing-list-2/

About Shéa MacLeod

Shéa MacLeod is the author of urban fantasy, post-apocalyptic, scifi, paranormal romances with a twist of steampunk. She also dabbles in contemporary romances with a splash of humor. She resides in the leafy green hills outside Portland, Oregon where she indulges in her fondness for strong coffee, Ancient Aliens reruns, lemon curd, and dragons.

Because everything's better with dragons.

Other Books by Shea MacLeod

Sunwalker Saga
Kissed by Darkness
Kissed by Fire
Kissed by Smoke
Kissed by Moonlight
Kissed by Ice
Kissed by Eternity

Sunwalker Saga: Soulshifter Trilogy
Fearless
Haunted
Soulshifter

Sunwalker Saga: Witch Blood Series
Spellwalker (Spring 2015)

Dragon Wars
Dragon Warrior
Dragon Lord
Dragon Goddess
Green Witch
Dragon Corp (Spring 2015)
Dragon Wars- Three Complete Novels Boxed Set

Cupcake Goddess Novelettes
Be Careful What You Wish For
Nothing Tastes As Good
Soulfully Sweet
A Stich in Time

Omicron ZX
Omicron Zed-X: An Omicron ZX prequel Novellette
A Rage of Angels

CPSIA information can be obtained
at www.ICGtesting.com
Printed in the USA
LVHW031540250219
608678LV00003B/540/P

9 780985 450694